# Midnight Hour

## DISCARD

Mary Saums

Hard Cover ISBN: 1-57072-107-6
Trade Paper ISBN: 1-57072-123-8
Copyright © 2000 by Mary Saums
Printed in the United States of America
All Rights Reserved

1 2 3 4 5 6 7 8 9 0

# ACKNOWLEDGMENTS

Many thanks to my husband, Lee Saums, for his patience during the writing of this book, as well as to all who gave time and encouragement to me, in particular: Lex Tinsley, Justine Honeyman, Linda Roghaar, Sara Ann Freed, my Harem sisters Ava Aldridge and Cindy Richardson Walker, Charles May and Carolyn Householder of Bodacious Books, and the past and present Bodacious Mystery Writers—Del Tinsley, Faye Jones, Rai-Lyn Wood, Dee and Warren Lambert, Darlon Smith, Mary Richards, Mal Clissold, Jean Onken, and Lona Spencer.

With very special thanks to Deborah Adams and the Silver Dagger crew.

# CHAPTER 1

THE PHONE HIT THE FAR CORNER OF MY BEDROOM like a blast out of a shotgun. Its plastic parts slid down the wall and fell in a heap. After a few seconds of quiet it sputtered a final electronic cough, then flat-lined like a dead man's monitor.

"You deserved a slower death, you demon tool of iniquity!" I yelled. I tugged the straps of my push-up bra, part of a fancy set I'd bought specifically for the evening—a truly joyous occasion. It was my fortieth birthday.

The dial tone was driving me crazy. I stomped across the room and slammed the receiver onto what was left of its cradle. Sitting down at my dressing table, I rubbed my face and tried to calm down. *To hell with that jerk,* I thought. I shook my new bottle of age-denying makeup and slathered it on.

Much to my surprise the debris-that-once-was-my-phone rang. Smacking my hands down, I pushed off from the dresser and picked up on the second ring. The mouthpiece hung by a few colorful wires. I stuffed them back in the handle, holding the chipped black disc as I hollered into it.

"Lewis Ray Stanton, I am still pissed! Don't call back, because I won't be here. Just because you broke our date AT THE LAST MINUTE doesn't mean I'm going to sit here by myself and turn forty all alone in this dump."

I took a breath and listened to the silence on the line. A throat cleared. "Um . . . is this Ms. Willi Taft?" a meek voice said. "Ma'am, this is Harlan Dobbs. I'm calling to ask if you'd like to buy tickets for the Fireman's Benefit concert again this year. Have I caught you at a bad time?"

"Not if you're single," I said.

"No, ma'am," he said, laughing. "Married and three kids. Now about those tickets—"

"In your damn dreams, fire boy!" I yanked the cord out of the wall, picked up the phone's remains, carried them to the kitchen, and chunked them into the trash. I needed a cigarette.

"Buddy! Here, boy," I called.

After I quit smoking, a friend of mine taught Buddy, my golden retriever, a new trick. Now anytime he sees a pack of cigarettes, he hides them from me. I've found them all over the house—behind pillows, stuck in flowerpots, in his toy box.

"Buddy, bring mama a cigarette," I said. He looked at me and whimpered. "Please, sweetheart," I whimpered back. "It's an emergency." My boy hopped off to sniff out a pack.

Behind me, I could see out my bedroom window in the makeup mirror. I scooted it over a tad to get a better angle. Parked across the street, the grill of a '68 Malibu was barely visible but still there—just as I expected.

Someone had been following me. He thought he was slick but I marked him right off. I'd been letting him run like a fish on a line all day. Since my birthday plans were ruined, I decided it might be fun to reel him in. I pumped my mascara brush, caked on a few layers of Darkest Black, then spritzed on my most alluring perfume as a little extra bait.

Buddy came in the bedroom with a slightly soggy pack in his mouth. "Sweet boy," I said and kissed him on top of the head.

I opened the closet door and went straight for the emerald mini-dress. It was low-cut and matched the green of my lingerie ensemble perfectly. I zipped it up, lit a cigarette, and cut my eyes out the window as I stepped into high heels. Before turning off the light, I threw my derringer in my purse.

"Tonight you are *mine*, you lowlife," I said. "Whoever you are."

After a few puffs and a few miles I calmed down. I felt bad about the fireman and promised myself to call back the next day. I'd apologize and buy some tickets.

It's not like me to lose it. Normally I have a calm, pacifist nature; but for several months, careening and sliding toward the Big Four-Oh, I'd been going through some weird personality changes. I kept telling myself the problem was my personal life, or rather my lack of one. Over the six years since my husband, Pete, died in a motorcycle accident, my relationships had been few, far between, and very brief.

As I drove, I began to see something deeper going on inside my head. I wasn't satisfied with any aspect of my life at a time when I thought I'd have it completely together. I had expected to love my work forever. For Pete to always be here. That we'd have kids, grandkids, the works.

Instead all I had was my career and my dog. As far as work, I was lucky. I'd been able to make a living as a studio singer, doing leads and background vocals on recordings for over twenty years. A dream job, many would say, here in Music City—Nashville, Tennessee.

Lately, it had been more like a nightmare. The older I got, the harder it was to make myself go to a session. Besides the strain of always being peppy and upbeat, it's tough sometimes to deal with showbiz personalities. Many times I've wondered if my life wouldn't have been much happier if I'd done what Mama wanted—become a music teacher. I did get my master's degree in music at her insistence, but never used it. Like I said, I got lucky early on in the business and made good money, which was my problem now: it paid too well to quit.

From the beginning, I've also had one other tiny problem—I hate country music. I mean I *really* hate it. But what could I do? Country sessions account for eighty percent or more of my income, with the remaining twenty percent coming from my first love, rhythm and blues.

As a teenager, my dream was to be a female B. B. King. I wanted to tour the country fronting a cool blues band in nightclubs, make the crowd go home smiling and crying. Instead, I wound up in Nashville. Believe me, you don't know what hell is until you've had to stand for six hours, listening to bad country songs over and over again while some nasal cornpone squeals like a pig in your ear. And you have to harmonize with it. For me, the thrill was definitely gone.

Luring the Malibu into the open was the only fun thing I'd done in ages. It's strange—I wasn't a bit scared. I rolled the window all the way down, took one last drag off my cigarette, and flipped the filter out into traffic.

He stayed a couple of cars back. After crossing West End, I slowed to be sure he saw me turn in at Dalt's, one of my favorite restaurants.

Inside I pushed through the bar crowd and found an empty seat at the far end. Through the plate-glass windows, I saw him park in front. He waited a few minutes before opening his door. I couldn't see his face but followed his jeans and boots up the sidewalk.

Turning my back to the door, I pretended to watch the TV above me. I waited a while, then found his legs midway down the bar beside two old lushes. It wasn't long before he sat between them, letting them cackle in his face and rub his back.

The bar stayed crowded as I waited patiently for the two-for-one drafts my stalker had ordered to do their trick. When he pried himself from the lacquered nails of his new friends, he walked behind me then past the low counter facing the kitchen.

I gave him a few seconds, ground out my cigarette in the ashtray, and followed. With one finger, I pushed open the glass-etched door that said MEN.

He was standing at a urinal minding his business. My plan was sketchy at best, but I knew now was the time to act—while I had the element of surprise and he was in a somewhat weakened state.

I didn't look. I thought about it but couldn't afford the distraction. Instead I walked up behind him, took out my gun, and stuck it in his rib cage.

"Hold it right there," I said.

His body stiffened. "I—"

"You stand just like that." I wasted no time and began patting the back pockets of his jeans.

"Hey, that tickles. You know, I'll let you do that without

the gun—"

"Be quiet," I said in my most commanding voice as I pulled out his wallet. I did a double take on his driver's license picture, thinking at first he'd replaced it with one of Mel Gibson.

"Sam Robbins," I read and flipped through, stopping on another ID card.

"A private investigator's license? Don't tell me someone paid you to follow me." It never occurred to me he was a professional. I have nothing. I *am* nothing. It was ridiculous.

"Answer me!" I said, pushing the gun in farther.

"Sorry . . . what was the question?"

Still looking through his wallet, I found a receipt for a roll of film with the name *Brenda Stanton* scribbled at the top.

Slinging the wallet down, I stepped back. Deep in my brain, the truth rattled around and finally tumbled out my mouth. "Lewis . . . is married?"

Sam slowly started lowering his arms.

"I told you not to move!" I said, feeling my eyes heat up and begin to water.

"Hey, give me a break. I just want to zip up my pants," he said.

I blew out a long breath and let my arm fall to my side. "I can't believe it. He didn't act married."

I heard a zip, and Sam Robbins, Private Eye, slowly turned to face me, his hands in the air.

"I take it you didn't know. I'm sorry," he said. He inched toward me, his palms out, with a strained look on his face.

"Oh." I shrugged, realizing he was looking at the gun. "Sorry." I threw it back in my purse. "That was in case you were a serial killer."

Sam spoke softly. "If it's any comfort," he said, "you weren't the only one." He bent to pick up his wallet.

"Only one what?"

"You're the third one I've followed. He's a popular guy."

*Good God a'mighty*, I thought, *I've officially hit bottom.* With my head spinning, I heard the laughter of women from all over the world bouncing off the tiles as if they were crowded in the men's room with us, welcoming me to a very old club.

Lewis and I only had a couple of dates. Part of the reason for my bad mood was I'd hoped, being my birthday and all, that tonight was the night. I tried not to count the years since my last close encounter.

"I need a drink." I wiped under my eyes and pushed through the door. Back at the bar, I scooted my stool up and leaned forward to flag down the bartender.

"Can I buy you a beer?" Sam asked.

We stared at each other a long time. I looked around his shoulders to the two lushes.

"Maw and Grandmaw's wanting you to come home. See how pitiful they look?" I said, pointing down the bar.

Sam didn't turn around. He just kept staring at me.

"Go on," I said, "they look like they just got your draft notice." I realized the two women were probably only forty-ish—*my* age now, I reminded myself.

"Another beer?" the bartender asked Sam.

He nodded. He had an honest, rugged face. The kind a girl could really relax in. His body was perfect. The kind a woman could—

*'Scuse me! Whoa, girl! Hang on to your panties, sister!* I heard as all those imaginary women stampeded out of the men's room. *He does look good—Yes, he does—Just like Stewart—And Mike—He's probably like them inside, too—Selfish— Thoughtless.*

Sam picked up his beer. He lightly clinked my glass with it and turned his beautiful, soulful eyes to mine. In a soft voice, he said, "Happy birthday, Willi."

The sharp intake of a hundred breaths preceded dead silence. *Woo! Well, excuse me—Like I said, he's perfect—Go ahead on—He's fine, girl.*

And I had to agree. I swallowed hard, gritting my teeth, but couldn't prevent a big tear from rolling down my cheek. It's pretty pathetic when someone you trust turns out to be a slimeball, and a complete stranger is not only nice, but wishes you happy birthday. *Well, hell*, I thought, *I guess I should say something nice back.*

"You're not very good at following people," I said. "What kind of investigator would think nobody would notice a classic 1968 Malibu?"

His face lit up. "I knew you'd like my car."

"Oh yeah? What else do you 'know'?"

He sighed like he didn't want to tell me. "Okay, your first name is Wilhelmina."

"Stop laughing."

"Sorry. Let's see—you're a singer. You lived in Muscle Shoals, then moved to Nashville in 1984. Married in 1987." He paused, probably wondering whether to skip over Pete's accident.

"I'm impressed," I said. "So what's your story?"

He was from Texas, which explained his legs. His parents died in a car wreck when he was twelve. He came to live with his only relatives, an uncle and aunt, in Nashville. He joined the Navy and roamed around the country afterward, settling in California. About a year ago, he came back to Nashville and worked in his uncle's pawn shop on Charlotte Avenue. Since the upstairs of the building was empty, his uncle let Sam use it rent-free. The two of them renovated the upper floor, making Sam an office with an adjoining apartment.

With the idea of putting his electronic and photographic skills to use, he became a private investigator. He wanted to attract the west Nashville divorce cases, including Hillwood and Belle Meade, two well-to-do neighborhoods. He figured he could make a good living when the inevitable occurred: the middle- to upper-class bankers, lawyers, etc. were able to afford mistresses and/or get divorced.

We talked so long I lost track of time. When his friends down the bar got up to leave, Sam went to say good-bye, kissing them and giving each a business card before returning.

"You know, Willi, that looks like a dancing dress to me."

"Sorry, cowboy. I'm not the country line dancing type."

"Not that. *Real* dancing." He threw some bills down on the counter.

"There's no such thing around here," I said.

He smiled and took my hand. Did I mention he had a beautiful smile? When I slipped off the stool he twirled me around into his arms. He squeezed me closer and began to sing in a mellow baritone, "Oh . . . how we danced . . . on the night . . . we were wed."

We waltzed down the length of the bar. The hostess opened the door as Sam snapped our arms out in a dramatic tango exit.

When I saw we were driving west toward Belle Meade, I said, "Wherever we're going, we don't belong there."

He grinned. It was a grin I bet he'd used to get his way since he was six years old. "Relax. They love me," he said and winked.

We turned into a strip mall of expensive stores on the edge of Belle Meade's business district. Although the shops were closed, cars were parked at the far end where one large building was still lit.

Sam led me down the sidewalk and inside the lobby of the Richland Dance Club. Gold glittered all around us in display cases full of trophies with dancing figurines on top. Seeing Sam, a woman at the reception desk rose and came to meet us.

"Hello, gorgeous," she cooed, her arms stretching out for a hug and a kiss. It was the first of many, expected by every woman we passed that night.

A silver-haired lady, who could easily have been a linebacker in her youth, saw Sam from across the room. She pushed through the crowd and gave him a loud smack on the lips.

"How's my sweet precious?" she said, pinching his cheeks. She wore enough hardware to set up a jewelry store, and her perfume, expensive and pungent, had the stopping power of a stun gun.

"Willi, may I introduce Douglas Anne Pennington, a friend and valued client," Sam said.

"Hello, dear," she said in a deep alto. She gripped my arm

just above the elbow and squeezed until I thought it would fall off. "I love this man; he saved my life!" She shook me, emphasizing each word. Leaning closer, she whispered, "My divorce. Sam got the goods on that rat-of-a-husband of mine." Her face brightened. "*Ex*-husband, I should say."

"Everything's final now?" Sam's voice was almost drowned out by the music blaring over the speakers. His arm was pulled behind him as a leggy instructor led him out to the floor.

Douglass Ann called out, "As of yesterday, I am a free woman!" Sam, now in the current of dancers, was out of earshot, so she turned to me. "In all my thirty-four years of marriage," she said, "I've never seen my husband so angry as when the judge ruled. His face turned blood red—it was so wonderful! As we walked out of court, he said, 'Doug, I'll kill you before I give up the condo in Destin.' Poor baby! No more love nest. I laughed the rest of the day! Excuse me now, dear. Relax and enjoy yourself!"

She pushed her purple see-through sleeves up, walked over to a little man half her size, and shoved him ahead of her onto the dance floor. Before he knew what was happening, he was clasped to her ample bosom and doing the cha-cha—with Douglas Anne leading, of course.

I couldn't keep from laughing. I looked across the room just as Sam caught me smiling. He spoke to his partner and released her with a swirl, then made his way back to me.

"I saw that," he said. "Careful, or you might have a good time. Stop trying to hide it." He pulled my hands down away from my mouth. Slipping his arm around my waist, he guided me out for a crash course in ballroom dancing.

For the next two hours we rumba-ed, samba-ed, and -foxtrotted. I had only a fuzzy recollection of how I came to be there—something about a frog named Lewis way back once upon a time. Sam's body was tight and strong. Being close to him made the rest of the world seem far away. As the music faded at the end of a slow number, he leaned down. I closed my eyes as his lips touched my ear.

"You're beautiful, Willi," he whispered, moving us in the

direction of the door. "Let's get out of here."

Once inside the car, Sam drew me close for a kiss. "Willi," he said. "I realize we've just met. And that you don't know me very well. But I want . . . that is, I was hoping . . . "

Leaning my head back on the seat, I let out a long breath. It had been a long time, too long. Sam was gorgeous and I needed him. I imagined him falling to his knees in gratitude at the sight of my underwear.

". . . and I realize it's a lot to ask . . ."

I rolled my head toward him, blinking like a contented cat. "Yes, Sam?"

". . . I was wondering, would you consider . . . going to a funeral with me tomorrow?"

My eyes snapped open. "A *funeral?!*"

"It's just a little legwork for a client." He looked deep into my eyes and lowered his voice. "You'll come?" he asked softly as he touched my thigh.

I looked from his fingers to his eyes and back to his fingers again. "We'll see," I said. "I'll have to sleep on it."

# CHAPTER 2

THE NEXT DAY I knew my best friends would be ecstatic at the news I had a real man in my life. Instead, I had to dodge a flying lemon wedge and a few ice cubes and then cover my face and head against a flailing of microphone cords.

"Have you lost your mind?"

"She never had one."

"You better grow a brain before you end up d-e-d, dead."

Ah, yes, the comfort and support of loved ones. We had a ten o'clock session at Ju-Ju's, a small recording studio off Music Row. My assailants were my three oldest buddies: Jill Greer (the lemon freak), Luanne Nichols (the ice hurler)—both of them fellow singers—and the engineer, Catherine "The Great" Maguire, who menacingly tapped her palm with the aforementioned coils of cords.

We had finished the three songs we'd been booked on. With the producer gone to lunch, Jill, Luanne, and I were hanging out in the control room while Catherine made cassettes.

The four of us, collectively known as the Harem, had been friends for years. Each of us moved from Alabama to Nashville as our sessions increased up here. Jill and I had our first paying gig at a tiny studio in Muscle Shoals where Catherine was the gofer. Luanne came up a few years later from Birmingham. We gradually began getting more sessions, usually as a background group, while Catherine worked up into an engineer's position.

So it was no use pretending nothing was new with me. They could tell right away. Luckily I had sense enough to make them wait until after the session to get details of the previous evening. Jill pulled her waist-length blonde hair over one shoulder and started combing. "The thing is, if Luanne had come in here with this story, I wouldn't have any trouble believing it—"

"What the hell is that supposed to mean?" Luanne interrupted, her jaw full of ice.

"—because she's always doing some fool thing," Jill finished.

Luanne crunched the ice as she let her chair fall forward with a thump. As usual, her short, black hairstyle and her clothes, simple but well-made, made her look like she had just gotten back from Paris. She wore skinny-legged black jeans and red-hot lipstick to match her turtleneck.

With her palms turned up, she feigned innocence. "I am not. Your problem is you've been married all your life."

Catherine stood watching in her stubborn bull stance, a Taurus through and through. Her frizzy red hair curled loose to her shoulders. She wore glasses and no makeup and had on her studio uniform—jeans and a T-shirt. "Willi, admit it. He could be lying. He stalked you, then he turns on the charm and you—"

"He was being paid, Cath. I saw his license. I saw his business cards."

"They could be fake! Anyone can have cards printed!" Catherine peeled off the labels she'd been writing on and slapped them on a couple of cassettes. She stacked them, then folded her arms over her chest. "I have just two words for you," she said. "Ted Bundy."

I sighed. Usually, it was *me* telling *them* to be careful. Now in the light of day, I could see how I might have been a little hasty. But Sam was a gentleman. He was funny. It was easy to talk to him. He was different.

"And don't sit there thinking he's different," Jill said.

"That's exactly what every woman thinks right before a man she trusts slits her throat," Catherine said, ever the optimist.

"I wasn't thinking that," I fibbed. They all glared at me.

"If he's so great, let us meet him," Jill said, putting her

comb in her purse.

"Well . . . sure. Sometime I'll—"

"Today," she said.

"I can't. We have a date."

"Perfect! Before you go wherever you're going tonight—"

I stood up. "It's this afternoon. In fact, I need to go now."

Luanne spit a few ice cubes back in her glass. "Where's he taking you?"

"It's a funeral," I said, covering my mouth and letting my voice trail off.

Without moving their bodies, they looked to each other, then back to me. Catherine reached over and cut off the tape machines. "A friend or one of his family?"

"Uh . . . actually, I don't think he knew him," I said.

The uproar that followed included:

"Damn, what's wrong with you?"

"I told you he was weird!"

"What more proof do you need?"

I said, "It's not like that! He's on a case. He said he's investigating." But the more I said, the worse it got.

Catherine plopped down in her roll-around chair, took off her glasses, and rubbed her eyes and forehead. "Girl, I can't believe you're being so stupid. He must be awfully good-looking."

"Or awfully good," Luanne said. For once, Luanne, the dumb black-haired one of the bunch, had made an astute comment. The others got quiet and raised their eyebrows.

There was no use denying it. "It's true. He's undoubtedly the handsomest hunk of man I've ever seen."

"You didn't," Catherine said.

"No, of course not."

"There's a party on Music Row this afternoon," Jill said harshly. "You bring him over to SFI Records so we can check him out. No excuses, you hear me?"

"Yes, ma'am," I said and hurried out the door.

My legs felt frozen to the back pew at Woodbridge Funeral Home's chapel. Luckily I'd brought my sweater since my only

— 13 —

appropriate black dress was sleeveless. This didn't help from the knees down, however, and I silently cursed manufacturers of both the hosiery and air-conditioning industries.

"Tell me again why we're here," I whispered to Sam.

"I never told you in the first place," he whispered back.

As "I Enjoy Being a Girl" played in my head, I crossed my legs, folded my hands in my lap, and smiled sweetly as is befitting a docile creature like me. Better that than my first impulse—to slam a hymnal across his chest.

Mr. Mysterious was beginning to get on my nerves. I'd had time to think about my friends' perspectives on the whole situation. True to my seesaw nature, I decided maybe he was nuts after all.

We stood while the deceased was rolled out a side door to the hearse. All I knew about him was his name, Martin Schaefer Sr., which I read on the black placard in the hall, and that he died of liver cancer at the age of sixty-two. Judging from the eulogy, the preacher didn't know much more than I did. His short speech focused on Mr. Schaefer's brave career on the Nashville Metro Police force, although no specific heroic deeds were given. He was praised for his devotion to family, having been left a widower with two children to raise.

I looked up into Sam's face. He wasn't staring at anything in particular, but his expression was intent, as if he recorded every movement of the bereaved family and friends.

As the crowd filed outside, Sam and I walked behind one group, then another, as he inconspicuously eavesdropped. He looked good in his jacket, a nice blue weave that fit him perfectly. He nodded politely to a few people but spoke to no one.

At the cemetery, we stood in the back behind the family seated under a small tent. Mostly older men attended the burial—other retired cops like Mr. Schaefer, I figured. Both the daughter, Stephanie, and the son, Martin Jr., looked to be in their late thirties or early forties. Beside Martin Jr. sat his wife and two small children, a boy and a girl.

I looked over the graveyard as the preacher read scripture. Glancing toward the cars parked behind the hearse, I saw three men and the back of a silver-haired woman. They seemed involved with their own conversation and completely unconcerned with the burial service.

The woman turned sideways. Before I could step out of view, she saw me. She waved her purple scarf in big arcs toward me and Sam.

"Where does she think she is, a picnic?" I said from the corner of my mouth.

Sam struggled to keep from returning her smile. He gave her a wink instead, and Douglas Anne Pennington blew him a kiss over a pudgy bejeweled hand.

"Let us pray," the preacher said.

After the service, I noticed Martin Jr.'s wife looking at me. After she'd spoken to most everyone else, she walked toward me.

"Sam . . . Sam . . . ," I said, panicking. We hadn't gotten a story together about our reason for being there, should anyone ask. She was too close for us to do so now.

"Willi? Is that you?" she asked. "Don't you know me?"

Shocked to hear her say my name, I shook her hand slowly, desperately trying to remember where we'd met.

"It's Julie Rhodes—Julie Schaefer now."

"Wow! Julie! You look terrific! I didn't recognize you." I cringed, realizing what I'd said.

She laughed. "It's okay. Thank you. You haven't changed a bit since high school."

I couldn't believe my eyes. Julie, a schoolmate from elementary through twelfth grade, had always been . . . how can I say this . . . facially challenged. Not that the rest of us girls were raving beauties with our braces and pimples. The thing was, none of Julie's features matched the others. It was like God took a Mr. Potato Head box, shook it, and gave her the first things that fell out. Her ears were uneven so her glasses were always lopsided, her nose was crooked, and her eyes, usually hidden behind frizzy bangs, were two different colors.

But today, Julie was absolutely beautiful. Her hair, a gorgeous natural red, was cut in a becoming style. I guessed tinted contacts now made both eyes luminous blue.

"I went to our last reunion," she said. "Nobody recognized me then either, not since my nose job."

I was at a loss for words, although Julie seemed perfectly adjusted and comfortable with herself. "It's so good to see you," I said, "although not under sad circumstances. I'm sorry about your father-in-law."

As she smiled, tears began welling up in her eyes. "He was like my own father, and so good with the children." She turned to look back at her husband. He carried their little boy in his left arm. His young daughter leaned into his side and held his free hand. While we watched, he released the little girl and rubbed his eyes before picking her hand up again and squeezing it.

"Marty has held up well today. He and his dad were very close. So how did you know him?"

"Oh . . . ." From behind me, Sam's hand reached out to take Julie's. "Uh, this is Sam," I said awkwardly. "I'm with him."

Sam turned his smile on high beam. "So nice to meet you, Julie. So you and Willi knew each other in school?" he asked, changing the subject with a smooth turn.

Behind us, we could hear Martin Jr. talking to a retired policeman. "I guess I wasn't cut out for police work," Martin was saying. "Dad wouldn't have approved even if I'd tried. He practically hog-tied and dragged me to college." His drawl was affable and well-practiced, like someone who made friends easily.

Julie took the little boy from her husband's arm as Martin's sister walked closer. With a broad smile, Stephanie flitted from person to person in the crowd, touching them as she passed. She wore a long gauze skirt under a navy blazer. Her hair, straw-colored with gray streaks, was pulled back in a long braid.

She reached out to her little nephew. Stroking his fine white hair, she murmured, ". . . the most precious thing, the only thing . . . ," her voice a wisp that faded as she floated past us.

Martin Jr. and Julie traded looks. "My sister is—"

"She's an artist," Julie finished. "A dear, dear person. Just a little different."

Martin smiled. "She paints, sculpts. She also grows and sells herbs for local organic groceries." He looked quizzically at Sam before following his wife's gaze toward Stephanie, now talking to Douglas Anne.

"We're concerned about Steph right now," Julie said. "She's been living at home with Dad, taking care of him since he became so ill. I hate to think of her alone now in that big house."

I stood watching Stephanie and Douglas Anne. For such different personalities, they talked like old friends as Doug repeatedly gripped Stephanie's thin arms.

Doug looked up, saw me staring, and motioned for me to join them. We said our good-byes to the Schaefers and started to walk away when Sam pulled me aside.

"I see someone I need to speak to. Catch up with you later," he said. He stopped at a small gathering of men that looked like old cops.

Stephanie's eyes glistened as Doug introduced us. Although she didn't appear to focus on anything, she wasn't rude or out of her mind in grief. She spoke softly, very relaxed and friendly. I wondered if she'd been smoking pot or taking some other "natural" sedative as she drifted away to other friends.

"I didn't see you at the service inside," I said to Douglas Anne.

"No. I wasn't there." She pronounced the last word with two syllables, *they-yah*, in that special Southern accent only acquired with money. Running her finger under the purple sash around her waist, she said, "I just came for the good part—to see them throw him in."

She watched my face to see if she'd shocked me.

"You must have been old friends," I said, trying not to look surprised.

"Not really. I knew his wife. We went to Harding Hills together." Again, she watched closely to see if I took her meaning. She patted her stiff hair and said, "Poor Lucy. She really married down."

*What a snob*, I thought. Harding Hills, one of Nashville's oldest schools, was for girls only. I doubt its curriculum had changed much over its lifetime, that of grooming elite brats as mates for the next generation of rich white boys.

I looked away to see Sam walk to another group of men. When Doug saw him, she made a movement as if to adjust her glasses, then placed her finger beside her nose. Sam grinned and did the same thing, like a secret signal between them.

Doug giggled. "You're a lucky woman, Willi," she said. "I wish *I* was forty-five." With that, she tugged her purse strap tight on her shoulder and walked away.

After the funeral, Sam agreed to go to the SFI Records party with me. He didn't seem to mind when I told him the real reason—that Jill, Luanne, and Catherine wanted to check him out.

"It's okay," he said. "I promised to let a buddy check you out, too."

I smiled, but somehow that didn't sit well with me.

White canopies covered SFI Records' parking lot on Music Row. Long tables of hors d'oeuvres outlined three sides of the lot. The fourth side was a low wall of black speakers and sound system gadgets, with an opening in the corner for the entrance.

Today's gathering was a Number One celebration. These are frequent on the Row, with most companies using the opportunity a number one record gives them to do their two favorite things—party and pat themselves on the back.

Anyone who worked on the record could be there—the SFI staff, the record producer, the engineers, musicians, background singers, publishers and songwriters with a cut on the album, various radio programmers, and anyone else who could finagle his way past the bouncer at the door. In other words, just about everybody in Nashville.

It was four o'clock when we got there. The tent was

already packed like a can of slimy glass-eyed music-business sardines. I leaned into Sam and held on to his arm with both hands, amazed at the difference between him and the other men I saw as we walked in.

Sam was like a beautiful David, walking tall and straight, his face open and devoid of the layers of psychoses common among entertainment types. In only a plain white shirt and black jeans, he out-spangled the other men with their sissy hairdos, dark sunglasses, earrings, and countless other affectations.

When Jill and Luanne spotted us, I could tell from their looks that Sam was no longer a suspect. I watched them as Sam approached. Without seeing his face, I knew he had turned the charm on high already and was reeling them in like mesmerized crappie.

They couldn't keep their hands off him. They hardly took a breath between asking questions, one after another, back and forth. There was no topic left unraised, no subject too personal for their interrogation. All I could do was stand back and watch as Sam good-naturedly played along.

"As head of this Harem, I hereby declare—" Luanne began.

"Wait a minute," I said. "Where's Catherine?"

"Working," Luanne and Jill said together.

"Of course. Why do I still ask?" Catherine almost always ended up working when we planned something.

"As I was saying," Luanne continued in a louder voice, "I hereby declare Sam Robbins worthy of gifts, honor, and praise, and bestow upon him the official title—Sheik of the Week."

With that, the two of them kissed his right cheek, his left, and then planted a big one on his mouth. When he turned to me, red and orange lipstick smudges covered his face.

While I wiped the lip marks off, a hand tapped Sam's shoulder. A shadow passed over his face when he turned.

"Don't I know you?" the man behind him asked. "You look familiar."

Sam squinted his eyes and shook his head. "I don't think

so. Sorry." He suddenly looked like an innocent little boy. I knew he was lying.

The man with curly, shoulder-length hair rubbed his arm up and down Luanne's back. "It's been a long time, ladies."

I still couldn't place him. I tried to imagine him without all the hair, but nothing registered. All of a sudden Luanne and Jill yelled, "Oh, Rick!"

Jill let him go long enough to give me a shove. "Willi, you dummy, don't you remember Rick Crawford? From L.A.? Remember he worked for Jud Sherrill that first time we drove up to work for him? Remember, it was the night Luanne pulled her shirt off in front of all those guys."

"That was an accident," Luanne said, "and you know it. That was also the night Jill drank rum and coke the whole way back to Muscle Shoals . . . "

". . . just pulled her turtleneck way up over her bra . . ."

". . . in the middle of the night, drunk and singing, and she kept sticking her head out the window with that long blonde hair flying everywhere . . ."

". . . in front of the most influential producer in Nashville, who to this day refers to us as 'them strippers from Alabama.'"

". . . and would sit down just long enough to take another swig, then lean her head back out with that hair whipping the car door and her singing 'Against the Wind.'"

How could I forget? Guess who was always the designated driver whether I liked it or not?

"We haven't seen you in so long!" Jill said, still on a hugging spree. She was a toucher, especially when it came to men, and Luanne, having learned from the master, hugged Rick from the other side.

I swear they are the worst flirts on earth. This is why we've always had plenty of work. I don't deny it. I'm not proud of it, but there are worse ways to get sessions in this town.

"Where have you been hiding?" Luanne asked. "We haven't seen you in ages."

"I've been in L.A.," Rick said. "I'm doing a few projects for SFI, so I decided to move back here for a while."

"That's great, isn't it Willi?" Jill said while giving me a strained smile. "You remember each other, right?"

"Yes," I replied. "That's really great." I was about to shake his hand, but Jill glared at me and clenched her jaw. I modified the shake with a half-hug, then stepped back to introduce Sam. Without looking, I reached for his arm. My hand felt only air, so I turned around. He was gone.

I looked over the crowd and saw him at the punch line.

"Earth to Willi," Jill said. "Did you even hear? Rick's *producing* now and might have some work for us."

I raised my eyebrows, nodded, and smiled, rather than expressing my true feelings: *Big whoop-dee.*

He was giving us a smarmy grin like he thought he was hot stuff. His jacket was iridescent like a snake's skin. His jeans were so tight I'm surprised he could breathe. I rubbed my palm on my dress, feeling kind of greasy after touching his hand.

Luanne and Jill read my mind and gave me dirty looks. They doubled up on the ego stroking to compensate for me. I couldn't help the way I felt; I remembered he skulked around the studio like a little weasel on that first session. Of course, I reminded myself, that was twenty years ago. Like everyone else, Rick had probably changed for the better. I decided to cut him a little slack.

I looked around for Sam again but couldn't see him.

Rick brushed the hair hanging in his face to the side. "So, Willi," he said, "who's your friend? Is he one of us?"

His voice dripped with arrogance. It was all I could do to keep from slapping the curl out of his lip. So much for slack. I took a deep breath, managed to keep smiling, and just shook my head.

"Nope. He sure isn't," I said and walked off to find Sam.

# CHAPTER 3

"SO DID YOU SEE WHAT YOU WERE LOOKING FOR?" I asked Sam on the way home. He hadn't said much since the party, just concentrated on driving. Although this was smart, considering Nashville's traffic and dangerous road system, I was antsy, wondering if his mission had been successful or not.

He didn't say anything. We got off 40 West at the exit to 46th and Charlotte. I stared past him at the tall weeds and brush growing wild behind a chain-link fence under the interstate.

"Be patient with me a little longer, okay?" he finally said.

He stopped at the end of the ramp, crept through the intersection, and turned right into a parking lot. "I need to take care of a little business here, then we'll go to my place and talk."

When Sam parked, we sat facing a gorgeous building with shiny chrome accents that gleamed in the sunlight. Behind the windows I could see rows of gleaming steel and shiny black leather. Above it all, giant red neon spelled HAWG WILD with smaller lettering underneath, FINE MOTORCYCLES.

Sam left me in the car. As I sat there, I tried to reason my way out of a bad mood. Of course he couldn't talk about a case. His clients expected confidentiality. If I hired him, I wouldn't want him blabbing my business to anyone.

Sam took his time. I fidgeted.

The longer I sat, the more I wanted to touch those bikes. The sight of them flanked and leaning to the side in the window drew me in. When we were first married, Pete and I used to ride all the time. I realized I missed the feel of them. What was the harm in looking? Before I could stop myself, I was pushing open the metal doors.

Hawg Wild was no small-time sales and service operation. The showroom, big as a car dealership's, was cleaner than my grandmother's bathroom. Everything was high gloss. Covering the walls were posters of muscular men and women straddling ultra-cool road machines.

"May I help you?" a nice-looking man in jeans asked.

"Just looking. A friend of mine came in a few minutes ago," I said, my friend nowhere in sight.

"Sam?" he asked. "He went in the back to see Doris." He smiled, watching me run my fingers over seats and handlebars. "Sure you don't want to go for a ride today?"

I laughed and shook my head. "Is it okay for me to go back?" I asked, wondering if Doris was an old flame or, God forbid, a current one.

"Sure," he said. I walked to the back of the building and pushed through the doors marked SERVICE.

The shop was as clean as the showroom. Several bikes waited in line for the big hairy mechanic who stood nearby. Oil stains smudged his orange coverall and the tops of his steel-toe work boots. From the look he gave me, I'd say he was about two-hundred-fifty pounds of mean redneck that really didn't care for girls or strangers coming in his shop where they didn't belong.

Gulp. "I was looking for Doris?" I said meekly as I scanned the room.

The mechanic wiped his hands slowly on a rag tucked in his pocket. As he came closer, he studied me from head to toe. I felt like an alien oddball standing there in a dress, panty hose, and pumps.

"I'm Dorace," he said slowly. His lip curled up in a smile, reminiscent of a professional wrestler.

"Oh, sorry. I thought Sam was with you."

"He's outside," he said and waved his rag toward the back door.

"Thanks." I stepped quickly through the garage with my heels tapping on the concrete. When I reached the door, I could hear muffled voices on the other side, like men arguing. I glanced behind me to see Dorace watching, then kneeling down. Though I was looking at him when he dropped a large wrench in his toolbox, I still jumped when it crashed.

Sam stood in front of another man who, except for his business suit, was the spitting image of Dorace. On seeing me, the twin put his hands behind his back.

"Here you are!" I said. "Is this a great place or what? Hope I'm not interrupting anything." I could hear my overly bright voice squeaking and hoped it didn't sound as false to them as it did to me.

"It's okay," Sam said, coming toward me. "This is Horace Wilcox. He and his brother own the shop here."

Horace nodded and said, "Ma'am," while running a finger under his collar. "We'll talk later," he said to Sam.

Sam didn't answer. He took my arm and led me around the side of the store to his car.

He was quiet as we drove. We passed a playground behind an elementary school, then zigzagged through a couple of alleys. Sweat beaded at his hairline as we parked behind an old block building.

"This is my place," he said, suddenly cheery. "Time to meet the family."

We walked up the back to a security screen door. Sam unlocked it and ushered me down a narrow hall with thin carpet. We walked by a utility closet and another door with cheap gold stick-on letters that said RESTROOM. At the front end of the hall, a small sign nailed to the wall said ROBBINS INVESTIGATIONS, with an arrow pointing up a set of stairs.

Afternoon light flooded through the front glass door of the entryway, as well as through a big window in the adjoining room. They faced Charlotte Avenue, a busy thoroughfare that runs through downtown Nashville and west toward Memphis. We stepped through the connecting door, passing under the word PAWN.

Stereos, lawn equipment, and musical instruments crowded the shelves and floor of the one-room shop. An L-shaped glass case running the length of the room held smaller valuables, mostly jewelry. As we entered, a bell sounded, momentarily interrupting the piped-in music, a big-band oldie.

Behind the case, a door moved slightly. In its small square window, a face appeared, then a long arm pushed into the room.

"Hey, mister," Sam said, smiling. "You got any left-handed lawn clippers?"

The round man walking behind the counter laughed and raised up a hinged panel. "Where have you been, son?" he said, slapping Sam's arm. They traded a few mock punches that left Sam defeated and in a neck lock. From there, he introduced me to Uncle Ralph.

"Ralph, this is Willi," Sam choked out. Ralph immediately dropped Sam to the ground and reached out to take my hand.

"How do you do, ma'am," Ralph said, oozing charm. He smoothed a hand over his mostly bald head, hitching up his pants over a nine-month belly. Right away I knew he was the kind of guy who never met a stranger. I could see the resemblance to Sam, not just in his features but in his open face and his direct look.

After talking a while, I began looking closer at the jewelry case. A little farther down, Sam and Ralph studied knives and guns under the glass.

"Here. Take a look at this baby. Just got it yesterday," Ralph said. "By the way, how's that .357 working out for you?"

Sam took the gun from Ralph, turned it over, and looked through the barrel. "I've just shot it once."

My ears pricked up.

"It's okay, I guess," he said.

"Who'd you shoot?" Ralph asked.

I studied the cameras.

"Ah, some guy down on Broadway. The trigger pull is a little heavy, but hey—dead is dead, right?"

Wide-eyed, I turned. The two of them looked at me with poker faces, then burst out laughing. When he caught his breath, Sam asked, "Willi, have you ever shot that gun of yours?"

"Yes, of course," I said. They looked at me like they didn't believe me. "I have!" I insisted.

"Good. We'll go shoot together sometime."

"Great!" I made a mental note to look in the yellow pages, find the nearest range, and go practice.

A phone rang somewhere behind the walls.

"That's mine," Sam said. "Come on."

I waved to Ralph as Sam grabbed my arm, pulled me out the door, and dragged me upstairs. At the top of the flight he punched in a number on an alarm pad and turned the lock.

I followed him inside, panting as he reached over an old wooden desk and picked up the phone. He switched on the overhead light, an ornate monstrosity hanging by three chains from the ceiling. It lit a cozy office which, aside from the desk, contained a computer, two overstuffed chairs, a set of wooden file cabinets, a nice bookcase, and a small antique table with a coffeemaker on it. All very neat.

As Sam talked, he unlocked another door and pushed me through it. "Wait in here for a minute," he whispered and went back to his phone conversation, closing the door between us.

I set my purse down and wandered about the large apartment. The floor was like the outer office's, nicely polished wood with rugs placed just so. A comfortable couch sat between two end tables that matched the one outside, each holding an old lamp. Beside a floor lamp, one chair with an ottoman was within arm's reach of a bookcase crowded with magazines and books.

*He must have a maid*, I thought as I entered the kitchen. The old-timey single sink and appliances were spotless. I peeped into the refrigerator; it was spotless. The view out the window, which was offset from the sink, wasn't that great, just the backs of other buildings. I walked through to look out the front windows.

The afternoon rush hour starts early in Nashville, and Charlotte Avenue was already busy. Across the street was Richland Park Library with a little picnic area next to it. Out the side window I could see dragons and psychedelic swirls painted on the bricks of a tattoo parlor/junk store on the corner below.

Going to the office door, I couldn't hear Sam talking anymore, but through the opaque pane I could make out his shape seated at the desk. Listening closer, I could hear the light clacking and occasional beep of his computer. I tried the knob, but it wouldn't turn. I knocked.

Sam cracked the door open a few inches.

"Why did you lock me in?" I asked.

"I didn't. The door gets stuck sometimes."

"Hmm."

"I need to write something up while it's fresh on my mind. It'll just take a second. Make yourself at home."

*In other words, get the hell out of here,* I thought. After a few minutes, the office door creaked open. "You okay in there?" Sam asked.

"Yes."

"Willi," he said, stepping through the door. "I need to make one more call."

"To get permission to tell me what's going on?"

"Sort of." He turned to go back to his desk.

"Don't leave on my account. I'm going to the ladies' room."

I couldn't hear anything from behind the heavy bathroom door. I sighed and jerked my purse up to the sink to fix my makeup.

The shoulder strap caught on an old heater in the wall. Rather than gently unhooking my purse, I yanked it toward me. When I did, the heater pulled out from the wall and I saw something intriguing.

In the crack where there should have been wires, a piece of wood was flat against the back of the heating elements. Behind it the wall was hollowed out. Some brownish-gray objects with white on them were inside.

Carefully, I pulled on the heater frame, trying not to make any noise. Feeling down in the opening, my hand came out clutching three cassette tapes. On the top one the white label read "Guiness-#1."

I put everything back, then flushed the toilet while easing the heater in the wall. As I put on some lipstick, I thought what an interesting afternoon one could have if one were extremely nosy and left alone here.

Walking out to the living room, I overheard a little of Sam's phone conversation: ". . . really no hurry at this point. For all we know, there's nothing to find . . . yeah, well, I don't know what to look for either." He looked up at me and said, "She's beautiful. I think she can. Okay. Talk to you tomorrow."

Sam hung up and held his hand out to me. "Come here, you."

I sat in his lap. He drew me closer, took a deep breath, and in a sexy voice said, "How would you like to become part of the exciting world of private investigation?"

For the next hour, we talked. He insisted that going to Martin Schaefer's funeral had not been part of an ongoing case. He'd gone as a favor to a client who couldn't be there himself. I let it go at that, although I didn't quite believe it.

He didn't want to talk about Hawg Wild or the Wilcox brothers either. He wanted to talk about his agency, detective work in general, and how much he enjoyed being his own boss.

I laid my head on his shoulder. "I'm glad somebody has his stuff together." At Dalt's the night before, I'd told him a little about my disenchantment with the music business.

"I have a solution, you know," he said. "You never know when you'll get called on a session, right?"

"Right. But I'm usually booked a few days ahead."

"Okay, but you have a good bit of free time."

"More than I'd like," I said. "Work has dropped off for me this year."

"So what you need is a little work, in some area outside the music business, with a flexible schedule you can fit around your sessions."

"Is this a pitch?" I asked. I put my arms around his neck and kissed him on the cheek.

"Yes. I need help."

"Do you do this with all your lady friends?" I traced the brown curls behind his ear.

"Never." He crossed his heart and held up his fingers in a Boy Scout salute. "Actually I told a client how you held me at gunpoint in the men's room. He wants to hire you for a job."

"Ha! I don't think so. This was your secret phone call? I can't do that; I'm not qualified."

"I'll qualify you. Look, you're bored. Your work isn't a challenge anymore. You're ready for something new, and I think my friend is right—you're a natural. We'll go one step at a time, okay? Just think about it."

That night, he cooked for me. As I watched him work in the kitchen, I found myself laughing at his silly jokes and bad Three Stooges impressions. I relaxed, the way I did the night before at the dance club, and marveled at his willingness to put the day aside and give me all his attention.

*I could learn a lot from this guy,* I thought. *I'm sick of me. Sick of what I've become as a result of all the pretentiousness required here in Little L.A., the Nashville music biz.*

Up until Pete's death, I had been able to do it with no problem. But with him gone, it was hard to find the strength to keep it up. I hated the way I'd become withdrawn and too critical of others and myself.

In my mind, I closed my eyes, held out my arms, and let myself fall backward into his laughter, the smell of yeast rolls, and the soft light of the apartment—one that felt very much like home.

"A penny for your thoughts," Sam said, turning off the oven.

"A quarter for your shorts," I said.

"Sold!" he said. "But first, we eat. You light the candles, I'll pour the wine." He dimmed the kitchen light and put a white cloth over his arm. With a tweak to his upper lip, he began an imitation of a waiter, mumbling made-up French words.

He unlatched the odd-sized kitchen window and pushed it out. "Voilà, madame! Zee wonderful sights and sounds of Par-ee!"

I looked out over the alley. No lovers kissed on the street. No lilting accordion music wafted up, only the evening traffic noise from Charlotte and the interstate. The closest thing to the Champs-Elysées was 51st Avenue stretching back to the horizon.

"Great view of the Arc de Triomphe," I said, pointing to the big green reservoir at the oil refinery.

Hearing the tinkle of glasses, I turned. In the candlelight, Sam gave a curt bow and clacked his heels together. With a wave of his hand over the table, he said, "Eet eez to your liking, yes?"

I sat in the chair he pulled out for me. The plate he'd fixed looked like it had been prepared by a Cordon Bleu chef. Gently lifting my fingers to his lips, he French-kissed the back of my hand.

All I could do was whisper, "Oh, yes."

# CHAPTER 4

MY HANDS TREMBLED ON THE WAY to my first solo stakeout. Well, *sort* of a stakeout. Sam said it was just practice. It had been a week since he first asked if I'd like to try out detective work. It seemed like no time.

Sam and I had been together almost every minute since then. When we weren't typing up reports, we cruised every sector of Nashville. Mostly I listened as he pointed out certain areas where he'd worked on cases. I hardly took my eyes off him the whole time.

He bought me a camera from Uncle Ralph (he'd become my uncle, too) and taught me to develop my own film in a little lab on the third floor above his apartment. The room upstairs was huge with no dividing walls from the front to the back of the building. It was empty with only some storage boxes stacked near the stairway opening. He'd built a make-shift darkroom around an old sink, and strung clotheslines across it for drying photos.

We did all kinds of things together that week. Uncle Ralph owned a few small houses he rented out in Sylvan Park, the neighborhood nearest his pawn shop. One day, Sam and I helped him paint and clean one that had become vacant.

I took Buddy with us and had a hard time making him leave. The fenced backyard had several big shade trees. He thought he was in dog heaven after living in a condo since Pete died.

"You ever want to get rid of this scroungy mutt, you let me know," Uncle Ralph said. He rubbed Buddy's belly and then tossed a stick toward the back gate. The breeze ruffled the leaves overhead, dappling the sunlight over the patio where Sam stood, hammering on the door frame. He had paint on his hands and raggedy jeans. When he saw me staring at him, he wrinkled his nose and smiled. I don't know if I've ever been happier than I was at that moment. I sank deeper into this new world, one I never would have found if not for that jackass, Lewis.

But as I drove through Sylvan Park on the way to my first assignment, I felt no such euphoria. Curving through the golf course toward West End, my heart rate went up as the reality of my new part-time endeavor drew nearer. I wiped my palms more than once on my pants legs, trying to remind myself this was no big deal.

The plan was simple: watch a house; if there was any activity, it would be by someone I had met and would have no trouble recognizing.

The house belonged to Martin Schaefer, the dead guy. His daughter, Stephanie, lived there. I found it peculiar Sam chose it for me to spy on. When I questioned him, he said he just thought it would be a harmless exercise.

My mission was to watch the house from 3:00 P.M. until 6:00 P.M., then go back to the office and write up a report. Since I had to be at Ju-Ju's for a session at seven o'clock, I decided to pick up something to snack on, and pulled into the Mapco at West End and Kenner, the street where Stephanie lived.

I backed out of the door carrying an armload of chips and cookies, a large coffee, and a couple of magazines.

"You must be awful hungry."

I looked over my shoulder. A smiling redhead took the coffee and magazines out of my hands. "Here, let me help you, Willi."

It was Julie Schaefer. I still wasn't used to her new face and hair. As we laughed, I fumbled with my car keys and opened the door. I almost dropped them when I saw Stephanie get out from the driver's side of her car and walk over to us.

"You remember Stephanie?" Julie said.

"Ah . . . ," I stammered, trying to look innocent and hoping one of Stephanie's New Age talents wasn't mind reading.

— 32 —

"Yes, of course. How are you?"

She smiled serenely, smoothing back some wild strands of hair hanging loose from her braid. As she looked over my junk food, I half-expected a reprimand, or at least a remark about the benefits of fruit and spring water. What she said came as a complete surprise. "Please tell Sam I miss him. He was such a comfort to Dad."

With that, she touched my arm and went into the store. I couldn't move for a moment, trying to grasp what she'd said. Julie spoke what I was thinking.

"I had no idea she knew Sam. She didn't mention it at the funeral, did she?"

"I don't know," I said, trying to remember that day. "I don't think so."

But I knew she hadn't. And Sam had certainly given the impression he'd never met Stephanie or her father.

"I'm hoping this weekend will help her," Julie said. "She's leading a few workshops out of town on Herbal Medicines and Crystal Powers or something off-the-wall like that."

"She'll be gone all weekend? I mean, that would be good for her. It sounds like." *I'll never make it as a detective*, I thought, *if I behave like a four-year-old who can't keep a secret.*

"Yeah. She knows most of the other speakers from previous fairs, so it should be a good thing for her. That's where she's headed now, after she drops me home."

In the back of her car, I could see a couple of lightweight carry-on bags in the floor. I sat in my car a while, wondering what to do next. I fiddled with my coffee and my purse until they left. As the hatchback pulled away, I read the bumper stickers promoting peace, the legalization of marijuana, and random kindness.

I decided to go on as planned to my rendezvous point, the last business building on Kenner before the residential section. I parked in its lot facing south down the street toward the Schaefer house, where I could see its driveway and front porch.

Immediately after turning off the engine, I reached for my

legal pad and began writing down the encounter with Julie and Stephanie. One of Sam's rules was to record everything on a case as soon as possible, before your mind reinvents what happened. I kept an eye on the house but felt fairly confident there would be no action there.

It gave me time not just to write up my report but to think about what Stephanie had said about knowing Sam. Why hadn't he told me he knew her? Or her father?

I let it all swim around in my head. Although I could think of no good reason to do so, I came to the conclusion that perhaps Martin Schaefer Sr. himself hired Sam. But how Sam would give a final report and collect his fee from across the great divide was beyond me.

At 5:45 P.M., after staring at the house for almost three hours, not so much as a squirrel had moved in the front yard. What was left of my coffee was cold. My lap and the car seat were dotted with cookie and potato chip crumbs.

I began stuffing wrappers into a trash bag and brushed all the crumbs I could into it. Most went in the floor. I crammed the bag under the passenger seat. When I sat up straight, I gasped and clutched my chest as a strong arm grabbed me through the window.

It was Sam.

"Having fun yet?" he said, laughing while I recovered.

"You scared me to death. What are you doing here?"

"Just checking on you. See any suspicious characters?"

"Besides you? None," I said. "However . . . ."

I told him about running into Julie and Stephanie, and how the house was to be empty for the weekend. He smiled and tried not to look too impressed.

"Good work. Tonight we'll celebrate your first successful stakeout. My place? After your session?"

"I'm not sure how long it will run. We probably won't get done before eleven o'clock. Why don't you come over to my house? Here, I made an extra key for you."

He looked at it a moment before giving me a kiss. "I have some work to do tonight. But I'll be there when you get home. Maybe I'll take Buddy on a late walk."

After another kiss, I backed out of my parking space. Turning left out of the lot, I looked in my rearview mirror. Sam waved to me from where he stood, making me wish I didn't have to work.

The session was a royal pain. Rick Crawford, the sleaze-ball we'd seen at the SFI party, had booked me on some demos. Unfortunately he chose not to book Luanne and Jill. It was just me and Rick's girlfriend, Shea Fleming, also from L.A.

As the night progressed, it became clear Shea had little experience (I suspected none) in the studio. I ended up singing and playing her parts on the piano so she could hear them. It wasn't the first time I'd worked with someone whose talents, although numerous and well-known to the producer, did not encompass the gift of music.

During a break, when Rick took Shea away to compliment her properly, Catherine and I sat at the console. It was already ten o'clock, and we had one more song to do. I gave her a disgusted look.

"Hey, I'm sorry," she said. "Rick said she was great."

"I have no doubt."

"I'll give her this—she looks good."

"Yeah, she does," I agreed. "Too bad people listen to songs instead of look at them."

Catherine groaned and twirled around in her chair. "You're acting mighty uppity tonight. What gives?"

"I don't know. I'm just tired of all this crap."

"Yeah, yeah. I know your real problem. You're in love. You've got the hots for that detective guy, don't you." It wasn't a question.

I sighed. "I need to call him while we're breaking. It looks like we'll be here a while."

She put her hand on my shoulder. "I'm happy for you. You deserve a good man."

"After the hard time you gave me?"

"What are friends for?" She slapped my arm and went for some coffee, leaving me alone to call Sam.

He wasn't at my house or his office. I left a message on his machine that I'd be home around midnight.

I was dog tired and bad tempered by the time I got to my condo. My mood didn't improve on seeing the windows dark and Sam's car not there.

When I got the door open, I dropped my purse and briefcase on the living room floor. I stumbled in the darkness, calling Buddy.

His answering barks were muffled. Shocked, I realized he must be shut in my bedroom, something I'd never done. I heard a noise in the hallway, and for a moment I thought Sam was there after all.

The next thing I knew, my back slapped down on the floor. All I could see was a dark figure rushing past me and out the door.

By the time I scrambled to my feet and looked, there was no sign of anyone in the street. I flipped on the light switch and reached for the phone to dial 911. When I hung up I realized what I'd been looking at while talking to the operator.

My house had been trashed.

I didn't know what to do with myself while Officer Stan Rowley and his partner, Officer Sondra Meadows, poked through my house. I kept walking and staring at the mounds of papers and books strewn everywhere. While I picked up my sofa cushions and fluffed them back into place, the two officers went into the kitchen out of my range of hearing.

I scanned the stereo cabinet. All my cassettes and CDs, once neatly stacked, now covered the living room floor like a big plastic rug. The stereo components had not been moved, and my TV—a small portable model—and VCR still sat undisturbed.

"Notice anything missing?" Officer Rowley asked, his heavy boots thudding from the kitchen onto the living room carpet.

"No." I went into the bedroom to check my jewelry box. I double-checked, making sure my two or three "real" pieces were still there.

In the extra bedroom, all the dresser drawers were pulled out. The closet door stood open. I started laughing, imagining the crook seeing it so packed with out-of-season clothes that he threw his hands up in disgust to search elsewhere.

Still, I put my hands out and dove into the clothes, parting them with one stroke. My fireproof lockbox was still there. Not much was in it—a few credit cards I rarely used. At least they wouldn't have to be canceled.

I shuffled back to the living room, where Officer Meadows stood at my desk. Her tall athletic body towered over me as I walked past. She turned on the banker's lamp there, and the light from it gave her dark skin a glow like polished mahogany.

"They were probably looking for money," she said. She had a no-nonsense attitude and a penetrating look that made me feel guilty in the silence that followed. I began to understand why people confess to crimes they didn't commit.

"Look, guys, I'm sorry, I don't know how to act. I've never had a break-in before," I said, flopping down on the couch.

Officer Rowley let the quiet stretch out a little longer. "From the looks of it, I don't think this was a break-in, ma'am."

"What do you mean? What would you call this?"

"There's no sign of forced entry. No windows are open or broken. The dead bolt on the kitchen door is locked. The front door wasn't jimmied. Assuming you didn't leave it unlocked, it appears someone used a key."

I started shaking my head, anticipating the next question but not wanting to consider the obvious answer. Sam was the only other person with a key. This *had* to be a break-in; the cops just haven't found the break yet.

The radio on Officer Rowley's belt squawked. He talked into it with numbers and strange codes as he stepped out to the front door steps.

"Two nights ago we worked another burglary that looked a lot like this," Officer Meadows said, closing her notepad. "Four doors down, at the end of the block."

"See? It couldn't have been—" I stopped, remembering the

sight of Sam's car in my mirror, hiding behind the bushes on the night we met a week before. *Surely not,* I thought. He couldn't have been watching in order to rob my house. It was a silly idea, but what if someone had seen him, written down his tag number? He might get in trouble for nothing.

"Couldn't have been who?" Officer Meadows asked.

In my mind, I heard the warnings of my girlfriends again. Could Sam have lied to me all this time? That very afternoon, had I not given him information on a house that would be vacant all weekend? I'd heard of thieves reading obituaries so they could find homes to rob. Had Sam been watching since Martin Schaefer's funeral, waiting for Stephanie to leave too?

"Ms. Taft, are you feeling all right?" Officer Meadows said.

*This is nonsense,* I thought. *Sam is a detective, not a thief. He's a great guy, one who wouldn't think such horrible things of a friend.*

"Let me ask you one thing," I said to her. "The other condo down the street that got hit, did it also look like there was no forced entry?"

"No. The kitchen window had been broken," she said.

I took a deep breath. Returning her steady gaze, I said, "Excuse me, I need to make a phone call."

While dialing Sam's number, I remembered I gave Jill a key when I first moved in. But that was the only extra.

I kept telling myself *Sam didn't do this* as his phone rang. Although I hadn't seen his face, I knew the intruder was shorter and smaller than Sam. The only other thing I could remember was the way he smelled, a mixture of sweat and the hint of citrus in his cologne.

On the fourth ring, Sam's answering machine picked up again. When it did, I collapsed inside. Trying not to break down and cry in front of the police, I bit my lip. *If I can just hold it together until he gets here,* I thought, *I'll be okay.* Wiping my eyes, I left another message.

"Sam, it's me again. Come over as soon as you can. Someone has broken into my house. The police are here now, and I really need you to hurry."

My arm shook trying to hold up the phone to my ear. I

was about to hang up when I heard a couple of clicks on the other end of the line. The handset clattered as I imagined Sam fumbling through his office door and then sliding across his desk to turn off the machine.

"Hello?"

"Thank God! Sam, sweetheart, listen. Someone was in my house when I got home, and he shut Buddy up in my room, and he pushed me, knocked me on the floor, and now my place looks like a cyclone hit it—"

"Whoa, slow down."

My throat tightened. I swallowed and tried to speak more slowly.

"Sorry, babe, I'm a little out of it right now. Please, just get over here . . . ." My voice trailed off. Through the haze in my brain, I realized Sam sounded strange. "You sound funny. Are you all right?"

When he didn't answer, I noticed the noise in the background. It sounded like several other people were in the room.

"What's going on? Are you having a party? Hell, Sam, leave them and get on over here!" Knowing I must sound like a hysterical bitch, I rolled my neck around a few times. "I'm sorry, I just need you. Please hurry."

"I can't do that."

This time, I knew what was wrong. This was not Sam.

"Who in the hell is this?" I said, feeling my anger rising.

"My name is Detective Joseph Bracken. I'm with Nashville Metro Police."

"Detective Joseph Bracken? Where's Sam?" I yelled.

Before he could answer, Officer Rowley grabbed the phone from my hand. He identified himself, then briefly explained my break-in. There were long, maddening silences that ended with Rowley's "No, sir" and "Yes, sir."

I ran into my coffee table as I backed away from him. He said a final "Yes, sir" and hung up.

"Ma'am, there's been some trouble . . . "

The pieces began to fit. A detective. From Metro.

". . . and we aren't really sure . . ."

In Sam's apartment at midnight.

". . . so we'd like you to come with us."

Bracken. The homicide hotshot.

"Ms. Taft?" Officer Meadows said, coming around in front of me.

I was frozen on the couch, numb with shock. Buddy jumped on the cushion beside me as I stared ahead. I held him close. He whimpered, not knowing how or why the world had ended, just that it had, and that he was there for me, to face whatever dark road lay ahead.

"They need to call Uncle Ralph," I said, my voice hardly a whisper.

Officer Rowley stared at me. "Bracken said he's already on the way." He motioned to his partner, a little jerk of the head telling her it was time to go.

"Can you tell me?" I asked him.

He looked at me a moment, his body motionless, his mind checking off proper procedures. "Detective Bracken will explain everything."

Closing my eyes against that confirmation, I felt myself rip down the center. It felt like half of me stood and looked back to see my other half still clinging to Buddy's fur. I looked around for my purse. It was slumped by the door.

When I put it on my shoulder, the weight of it made my legs buckle. I started to go out but turned back to the kitchen.

"Wait," I said. "I've got to feed Buddy."

I poured out some dry food. At the sink, I refilled his water bowl and stared out the window. Not even one small light flickered in the darkness. Summoning my strength, I turned to enter the big black nothing that waited. The new empty world. The one without Sam.

They took me to the Metro Police building downtown by the river. I'd never been in a police car. Any other time it might have been fun, but that night I couldn't have cared less. It was 1:15 A.M. and I was a zombie. Officer Meadows showed me to a chair facing her desk, then settled in behind

— 40 —

her keyboard.

Every few minutes she asked me a question, always something she already knew or was looking at in her notes. Maybe it was habit, a way of making sure she got things straight. But I got the feeling she did it to help keep me connected too, sort of like a nurse tapping you awake to keep you conscious.

I was surprisingly calm. The swirl of events and unanswered questions in my head moved so fast there was no way I could make heads or tails of anything. I let the incoherent chattering of it all float above my mind's reach and concentrated on the small area of what I did know, answering the officer's queries with a simple "yes" or "no."

Every few minutes I thought, *You don't know for sure he's dead—he might just be hurt.* I told myself it might only be a break-in, maybe at the pawn shop.

But I knew the truth. I knew Detective Bracken wouldn't be there for anything less than a murder. He was the force's heavy hitter and wouldn't be working on a small-time burglary.

After sitting another thirty minutes, fidgeting, standing to keep my legs from going to sleep, I heard some activity in the outside hallway. A group of five or six people pushed through the door at the far end of the room and moved in my direction. It was like watching an approaching tornado, the group like a cloud of debris surrounding a center of formidable energy, a tall, heavyset man who barked down orders into his wake.

Making a sharp turn at a room divider, he took off his jacket, hung it on a hook, and loosened the tie from around his thick neck. All his followers went off in other directions, all except one.

Waving a hand, he motioned to the young cop. I could read his lips as he said, "Have a seat, son." Officer Rowley did as he was told and sat very still as he talked. Every now and then the big man leaned back, straining the chair, and closed his eyes, rubbing them, his fleshy face, and his short graying hair. He listened intently, never interrupting, until the young man finished.

Officer Rowley looked over his shoulder toward me and Officer Meadows and said, "That's her." The big man looked up. His body tightened as he fixed his eyes on me. It was a look no part of my body will ever forget, the look of a grizzly assessing his prey.

Officer Meadows got up, took a sheet out of the printer, and put it together with the others she'd typed. She walked purposefully toward the two men, her steps not too eager, not too slow. If she was intimidated, she didn't show it as she presented my report. She stood by as Bracken scanned her work, the crispness of her black uniform and the perfection of her hair bun exuding a confidence that quietly defied anyone to find fault.

The man put the report on his desk as the two officers walked away.

"Sorry you've had to wait so long," Officer Meadows said, staring down on me. "Detective Bracken would like to talk to you now."

I walked to his cubicle. He stood, took my upper arm and hand as if I were an old lady, and guided me to the chair. In an instant he flipped from grizzly to teddy bear, telling me his name in a soft-edged voice and assuring me he wouldn't take up much more of my time.

When he settled back into his chair, he took up the papers again and pretended to look them over.

"So," he said, "someone was in your house when you got home tonight?"

"Yes."

"Didn't take anything?"

"No. Not that I noticed."

"You say he pushed you down, then ran out the door?"

"Yes."

"But got away before you could get a look at him . . . ."

His tone had a hint of sarcasm, as if he'd heard that one many times before. I didn't answer since it had not sounded like a question, and we sat looking at each other a while in a mini-game of chicken.

Bracken spoke first. "This says you got home around midnight. Do you mind telling me where you were?"

"I was working." I gave him the details of the session, not saying I'd seen Sam just before going to the studio.

He sat quietly, writing as I talked. His big frame heaved as he took a deep breath and let the pen clatter on the desk. Leaning back, he laced his fingers together and set them on his chest.

"I saw you the other day," he said, ". . . with Sam."

My mind raced, trying to decide what to say. I didn't want to lie about anything to the police, but somehow it seemed only natural to give away as little as possible.

"Where?" I asked, hoping to buy a little time.

"At Martin Schaefer's funeral. Did you know him?"

"No. I only went along because Sam asked me." I realized Bracken must have been one of the men Sam talked to at the cemetery.

Bracken started laughing. "That's right. He said it was your first date."

So he knew Sam. I wanted to ask so many things—how long had they known each other, but most of all, why was he at Sam's apartment and what had happened?

I wanted to smile, but my face was rigid with the tension of trying to hold myself together. I knew I couldn't last much longer. I was too tired.

"That was pretty cute, the way you pretended to be Sam on the phone," I said. "Why did you do that?" My voice shook a little, but I gave him my best tough-guy stare. "Is that how policemen get their kicks?"

He stared back for a long time, then reached into a drawer. The chair creaked with relief as he slowly rose. I began to regret my attitude as I noted his heft. I was an idiot to antagonize The Man. I was nothing but a little gnat compared to him, hardly worth swatting. He stepped around to sit on the edge of the desk in front of me.

"Here, take the box," he said as he handed me some tissues. I hadn't realized my cheeks were wet until then. I dabbed them dry while he took a cigarette pack out of his shirt pocket. He tapped one out and stuck it on his lip. Lighting it, he squinted as the smoke rose, his eyes never leaving me, studying me with what I can only describe as a tender look.

"Could I have one of those?" I asked.

He offered me the pack and snapped his lighter open for me. After I took the first puff, he said, "I was just doing my job."

We sat for a while, smoking in companionable silence as I returned his look. In it, we agreed there was no point in playing games. He could see I already knew what he had to tell me.

"Someone surprised him," he said. His voice was very low. "It looks like Sam opened his office door. Someone was probably waiting in the hall in the dark, and the guy pushed his way in with Sam."

He paused and took a long drag. "He was shot twice in the back. There was no sign of a struggle."

As I tried to grasp what Bracken described, I folded over, sobbing, hugging my knees. He let me sit a while before speaking again. "I wish I could tell you more, but that's all we know right now. What I want you to do is go home, get some sleep. I'll call you tomorrow."

I got up, not caring about anything, too tired to protest.

"I guess I need to call a cab," I said.

"No. I'll walk you downstairs. Someone will take you home."

We didn't speak in the elevator or in the halls. When we got downstairs, I noticed someone walking toward me. With his arms outstretched, Uncle Ralph came to me, looking ten years older than the day before. As he hugged me I felt him tremble.

Sam had been like a son to him. Having just lost him, I was amazed he had even thought of me or that I might need him. He must have waited in that awful station lobby at least an hour for me to come down.

"Did you take good care of my girl, Joe?" he asked. It was exactly something Sam might have said.

"Yeah. I was pretty easy on her."

"You better. I can still whip you, you know." Ralph sniffed and ran his hand across his face.

Bracken put his arms up. "I know, I know."

"Thanks, pal." They shook hands, and Uncle Ralph and I turned to leave. "I used to hang out with his big brothers in the old days," he said. "Little Joe was our favorite punching bag."

We had almost reached the doors when I felt a heavy thud on my shoulder.

"Don't go home." The bass voice was right above my ear, and the weight of Bracken's hand felt like an anchor. I looked up to see him deep in thought. He shook his finger in the air and asked, "Did Sam have a key to your place?"

"Yes . . . ."

"Don't go home. She can stay with you and Lucille tonight. Right, Ralph?"

"Sure, of course."

"Did your key have any special markings on it?"

"It has a red cover with my first name on it."

Bracken rubbed his chin. "I'll have a look through his belongings, make sure it's there. In the meantime, stay with Ralph."

He didn't wait for an answer but went quickly back into the heart of the police station.

"But what about Buddy?" I asked Uncle Ralph.

"We'll pick him up in the morning. Later this morning, that is. Come on. Lucille has lots of nightgowns, and the extra room is always ready for company. You stay with us tonight."

Walking out to his car, I kept my arm hooked tightly around Uncle Ralph's. I looked up into his face, round and sad.

"Everything's going to be all right, sweetheart," he said and kissed my forehead.

I tried to think of the right words to say, to thank him, to tell him how much it meant for him to be there.

But words weren't enough. The best I could do for him was let him keep busy, let him fuss over me if that's what he needed to keep his heartbreak at bay, even if it was just for a little while longer.

# CHAPTER 5

AFTER SAM'S FUNERAL, I promised Bracken I'd meet him at Sam's office. On the way there, I stopped at Uncle Ralph's, where I'd left Buddy for the day.

"Ralph . . . ." I didn't know how to begin. I wanted to find out if Bracken had told him anything new about Sam's death, knowing neither might tell me the truth if he thought it would hurt too much.

He looked at me, then put his arm around Buddy, who flopped to the ground and rolled over for a good belly rub.

I tried again. "Please. Tell me what happened."

For a minute, I thought he hadn't heard me. Then he shook his head. "Sweetheart, all I know is what Joe told us. That somebody with a gun surprised him and shot him."

"But why? Who would hide and wait to kill him? Who hated him so much?"

"Nobody. Sam didn't have an enemy in the world. Everybody liked him."

I thought it was pretty obvious he had at least *one* enemy but, out of respect, didn't say so. I stared at Ralph.

"What I'm saying is," he said, "no one that knew Sam would've killed him. It must have been a stranger."

"Everyone has enemies. Maybe he owed somebody money, or a jealous boyfriend of an old girlfriend of his."

"No," Ralph said, shaking his head as I talked. "Nothing like that. It was just a robbery."

I could understand that Ralph wanted to think that, and didn't want to push it then. Hell, I agreed—Sam was great. I couldn't imagine anyone would want him dead. But the truth was, I hardly knew him. And even Ralph had only been close to him again the last few years.

"It was the pawn shop," he said. "It had to be. Some punks were in there to rob the place. Sam came in on them. That's what I think happened."

"But if they were hiding from him—well enough to catch him off guard—why didn't they wait until it was safe to leave? It doesn't make sense."

"Sense don't have anything to do with it. Where is the sense in a sixteen-year-old having a gun, stealing so he can buy drugs? Pawn shops all over town get hit. It might be the same guys doing them all, it might not. The punks are all alike anyway, not caring if they hurt or even kill a man. Nothing matters to them."

His eyes watered over. I didn't have the heart to keep on. I got up and kissed his cheek.

As I left, I looked out across the yard. He knelt beside Buddy, who put his front paws up on Ralph's shoulder. Ralph wiped his cheeks with the back of his hand before getting up, and the two of them took a slow walk together around the inside of the fence.

A patrol car and another sedan were parked at the pawn shop. I made a sharp left, parking on the side street between the tattoo parlor and Ralph's building.

A small wreath hung on the door. The hall was dark. I put my hand on the rail and leaned in as I walked tentatively upstairs. At the first landing, I could hear movement further up in the office. Yellow barrier tape flapped on either side of it, stirred by the old window fan at the end of the hall. A broad back spanned the door frame, and big legs stepped backward as I creaked up.

Detective Bracken's bulldog neck turned to me. His scowl softened a bit momentarily around his eyebrows, then reset. My skin rippled with goose bumps. I squeezed the rail tighter.

"Thanks for coming. We won't take up much of your time. This is Detective Haynes," Bracken said, nodding to a man behind the desk. "We know it's upsetting for you to be here. Just look over the place again—see if you notice anything different."

I set down my purse and looked around. Some papers lay scattered on the floor. Through the door to the apartment, I could see books and magazines pulled out of the bookcase and thrown onto the rugs.

I glanced through the open drawers of the desk and flipped through the hanging files. They were a mess but so was my mind. I really couldn't tell if anything was gone or not. Taking out my handkerchief, I wiped my fingers, sticky from where the cops had dusted for prints.

"You know, I only worked up here a few days. I'm not sure I'd know if anything was missing."

Detective Haynes's eyes never left me. "Do the best you can," he said. "What exactly did you do for Mr. Robbins?"

"Not much. I helped him enter information from his case files into the computer. I did a few invoices and mailed them."

"But you did no investigations yourself?" he asked, pushing his glasses up.

"No."

Bracken stepped over. "Can you think of any problem cases he had, or clients who may have been unhappy with work he'd done for them? Anything like that?"

"No. Everybody liked him," I said, borrowing Ralph's phrase.

Standing behind the desk, Detective Haynes gave a crooked smile. His fingers began drumming on top of Sam's tape player.

*Oh man, I am slow,* I thought. My mouth fell open as I remembered the stash of hidden cassettes.

"Ma'am, are you feeling okay?" Haynes stopped tapping. "Have you thought of something?"

"No." I shook my head. "I just need to go to the bathroom."

I slid the bolt on the inside of the bathroom door and put my purse against it. While I waited to calm down and get myself together, I blew my nose.

Slowly easing the heater out from the wall, I peeped in. It was still full. Being careful not to make any noise, I emptied it out, putting the Guiness tapes from Sam's stash into my purse.

My knees were stiff when I finally stood. I took a deep breath, shouldered my bag, and prayed they wouldn't search me due to the guilty look on my face. As I walked out, I dabbed at my eyes with toilet tissue.

Detective Bracken stood blocking the door to the office. I twirled on my heels and sauntered in the other direction, trying to concentrate on the living room, glancing around to find anything unusual.

Seeing nothing, I looked up and caught Bracken in another grizzly look. He had relaxed it by the time I got up the nerve to walk over to him. Damn, he was hot and cold. He had been nice to me the night Sam was killed, but I still didn't trust him completely.

Sam had gone to a lot of trouble to keep those tapes hidden. Since he had taken such precautions to keep them secret, so would I. If necessary, I'd hand over anything pertinent to Bracken. Later.

"I know it's hard for you right now," he said, "but just talk to me for a minute."

My lips were dry. I licked them and swallowed.

"Yes, sir. Any way I can help."

He sized me up, looking as if he didn't much like what he saw. "What do you think about all this?" He gestured with his hands, palms up in the air.

I blinked. "About what?"

"What are your thoughts on the coincidence that someone was in your house the same night Sam was shot? It's odd, don't you think?" He smiled and scratched his head.

I shrugged my shoulders and just looked at him.

"Are you accustomed to burglaries, Ms. Taft?" His voice was edged with impatience, and his inflection hinted at knowing more than he let on.

"Of course not. But if you remember, my report said other break-ins—"

"Your report," Bracken interrupted, his words getting louder, "said there was no sign of forced entry at your condo. And nothing was stolen."

"Yes, but—"

"You told me yourself, didn't you, Ms. Taft, that Sam had a key to your place."

"Yes, he did. But that was not him in my house."

"You're sure about that? You don't sound like it." The tight clench of his smile seemed to hold in secrets as he put his lips together.

The image of Sam's car reflecting in my makeup mirror kept popping in my head. I didn't like the way Bracken talked, as if he could see that picture in my mind.

"Look, Detective. I don't know what you're getting at. It's a coincidence. A ridiculous, stupid coincidence. All I'm certain of is that Sam wasn't the man who pushed me down in my house."

I was breathing hard and hated myself for letting him get to me. My purse felt like it had four bowling balls in it. I had to remain calm and get the hell out of there.

"Plus," I said, "I doubt anyone who killed him would have a reason to come find me too, besides the problem of not knowing where I live just from my key."

He stared, his hand on the side of his face in deep thought, then nodded slowly.

"Yeah. I think you're right," he said to a spot on the wall. "Maybe I'm reading too much into this. You probably just forgot to lock your front door on your way out. Then you came home before the guy could steal anything." He turned and shuffled away, not waiting for any response. "You're free to go whenever you're ready."

I'd made it out of the office and was down a few steps when he called my name. He stepped out into the hallway and snapped his fingers.

"One more small thing. Did Sam ever mention Guiness?"

He waved a piece of paper that looked like a fax. I walked closer to see it. Except for one line at its center, the page was blank. It read: "You were there 7-25-78." The signature was one word—"Guiness."

I froze. Putting on my dumbest look, I turned and scrunched my eyebrows. "Guiness? I don't think so."

Bracken smiled and held up his hand. "Long shot.

Thanks anyway."

On the way home, I was unusually fierce in my comments about the driving habits of my beloved fellow Nashvillians. I found myself using cuss words in florid combinations. I was surprised to find an interesting side effect of my distress—I made it home in record time. Through all this, Buddy, who normally rides with his head out the window, opted for the backseat floorboard. He lay quietly there until we screeched to a halt in front of the house.

I wasn't sure why I was so angry. I think the last straw was Bracken's remark implying I was just a dippy broad without sense enough to lock her doors.

I fumbled with the key to the new lock Ralph had installed for me. When Buddy swished by, I slammed the door shut so hard, he ran for the safety of the bedroom.

The mess was still there. I could feel myself shaking as I picked up a few papers, unable to read what they said or even decide where to put them.

Outside, a loud bass rumble got louder and louder as a car full of rap aficionados thumped down the road. The angry staccato of the so-called singer punched and spit out hatred on the neighborhood. *They ought to put those ignorant little creeps in jail,* I thought, *for playing that junk so loud.*

I don't remember feeling the ceramic in my hand. The crash was muffled, barely registering in my head as a lamp breaking against the wall. Papers lying in drifts like snow suddenly dispersed and floated to all corners of the room. I don't even remember touching them.

I grabbed a pillow off the couch and hit every surface of every object in sight. With that done, I slung it away, fell to my knees, and pounded my fists on top of the coffee table. When they started to hurt to the bones, I shoved the table back and kicked it with both legs until it was on its side against the wall. With only enough energy left to fall over, I lay on my side and cried into the afghan on the floor beside me.

I woke up at 9:00 P.M. The bare bulb of one lamp that

escaped my wrath was still on. I got up, cut it off, and set its shade back in place. Stripping as I walked to the bathroom, I left my clothes where they landed.

My nose was stopped up and my head hurt. I had a session the next afternoon, so I took a big swig of cold medicine and brushed my teeth.

Buddy was on my side of the bed. I gave him a little nudge. While he yawned and stretched, I put on my sleep shirt before crawling in beside him, not caring if I ever woke up again.

# CHAPTER 6

WE ALL GOT TO JU-JU'S EARLY. While Catherine finished recording a guitar part, the rest of the Harem sat in the control room with her. I had my head propped up on my hand, staring out into space, when she slapped my arm out from under me.

"What are you thinking about?" she asked.

I looked around at my friends. They all had sad looks, expecting, I think, me to say something about missing Sam.

"Bear Bryant," I said.

A collective groan went up. Luanne said, "It's just July. Don't tell me you've got Tide on the brain already. You're getting worse every year."

I ignored them and pointed through the door's glass pane to the men standing in the hallway. We were working for a rough-looking gospel group from Cincinnati. The band members, a couple of roadies, and various other hangers-on lolled about in their country-western outfits. If I hadn't known better, I'd have thought we were at a convention of Hank Williams Jr. impersonators.

"What about them?" Jill asked.

"Hats," I said. "Remember Bear Bryant always wore his black-and-white-checked hat to games? And then, when they played under a dome, he wouldn't wear it because his mama taught him you don't wear hats inside."

The three of them stared at me.

"So?" Catherine said.

"So look at them!" I said. "What I want to know is, where was Mama? American society has flat gone to hell."

I caught Jill rolling her eyes at the others. "Willi, they've always done that. Nothing's changed. The world has not gone to pot just because Bear died."

I sighed. "Yes it has, too. These days men worry too much about how pretty they look."

Realizing I would sway no recruits to my side, I walked out to get a cup of coffee. It was dark in the small dining area, as it was all over the building with that 24-hour nighttime look that "mood" lighting gives all studios.

The gospel group's bass player, a tall, hefty guy, came over to the coffee machine as I stirred in generic white stuff. He had a strange look in his eyes, one peculiar to that sub-group of musicians who are both a) country music lovers, and b) churchgoers. It was a familiar leer that conveyed "Praise God!" and "Ain't I something?" with equal emphasis.

Airbrushed on his T-shirt was one of those fish symbols with Greek letters inside. Reptile skin covered his boots. My head came about level with his belt buckle, a huge slab of metal that said TRUCKERS DO IT ON THE ROAD.

I was sorry I smiled at him. When he walked behind me, he pinched what felt like a sizable chunk out of my rear end. Still grinning, I pulled away, grinding my heels into each toe of his boots. I did this purely for spiritual reasons, you understand, in order to help him do a painful, if not contrite, two-step back to Jesus.

"What's wrong with you?" Luanne asked as I stormed back into the control room.

"That guy just pinched me!" I motioned toward the hall where he'd already mingled with the other cowboys. I'd never have been able to pick him out of a lineup.

"Oh, you just imagined it," Jill said.

"I did not! These gospel groups are the worst."

"What a thing to say," Luanne remarked, taking offense.

I growled.

The tape whirred as Catherine rewound it. On the studio floor, the guitar player unplugged his gear. He took off his headset and immediately, irritatingly, put his hat on. When he got up, he looked straight at Luanne and gave her a little nod as if to say, "Howdy, ma'am. You sure are a purty little thing." He sucked in his belly and strode, crotch first, to the adjoining door.

Luanne hung her head and said, "Oh shit."

"Don't worry," I said. "It's probably just your imagination. A word of advice—don't stand up until he's gone."

The hall door opened at the same time Jerry, the guitar player, came in from the studio. He walked over, right next to Luanne, to listen to the playback as Rick Crawford came in from the hall.

Rick went into a sickening jive of how lovely we all looked, how great the guitar overdub was, and how fantastic the whole track sounded. We girls were immune to that sort of thing, but Jerry, being more of a road musician, was unaccustomed to such flattery and believed it all.

Rick reached into his leather bag and brought out a small folio. After he and Jerry exchanged business cards, he looked through the clear pages for an empty slot. As he flipped, one with a red logo caught my eye.

I smacked my hand down on the page, almost knocking it out of Rick's hands.

"You know Sam," I said, realizing the card was one of his.

"Sam who?" Rick asked.

I slapped my hand down a few times on the open book and pointed to the bright red lettering that said ROBBINS INVESTIGATIONS.

"Oh. He did some work for a friend of mine."

"Really? What friend?" It was a nosy remark, but I didn't care. After the torture I went through on that session with Rick's tin-eared girlfriend, I figured I owed him a little discomfort.

"Ah . . . well . . . ," he stammered as he shook his shoulder-length curls. "That's funny. I don't remember at the moment who gave that to me."

I nodded as we stared at each other, then returned his lie. "You know, I sure did enjoy working with you and Shea the other night. I hope you'll call me again."

"As a matter of fact," he said, "I do have another project coming up soon—another female singer. She's not as talented as Shea. But she's young, beautiful, and willing to give her all for her career. I predict big things for her."

"And lots of little bitty things too, poor child," I said, turning away.

The tape started rolling as Jerry scooted closer to Luanne's chair. He closed his eyes, reveling in the genius and mastery of his own guitar work. The intro was played in the style known as *chicken pickin'*. It sounds just like you might imagine, like somebody grabbed a chicken and pulled its feathers to make it cluck out a tune.

As the intro squawked into the first verse, Jerry opened his eyes, clearly pleased with himself. Rick waved good-bye from the door. When Jerry waved back, he let his hand drop down onto Luanne's shoulder. She jumped, taking only a half-second to move, then she followed Rick as he pushed through the twenty-odd Bocephuses in the hallway.

My mind wandered all through the session. Thank goodness my pals were there to take care of shoveling horse hockey back and forth with the producer and the band. I certainly wasn't up for it.

At least they were easy to please. The arrangements were simple. I think I could have gone to sleep and snored my part and no one would've noticed.

On the studio floor, Jill, Luanne, and I stood in the dark with just one small concert light on our music stand. Through the thick panes of glass, we could see Catherine and the producer seated at the console under a row of dim lights.

I took my headphones off and tried to rub away a headache that was gaining on me. The studio was quiet around us except for the muffled track playing low in my phones. Next to me, Jill leaned against a stool and sipped her lemon water. Luanne half-hummed as she listened and stared at the floor.

Inside the control room I could see people talking and moving around but I couldn't hear anything. I glanced around the studio at what were familiar surroundings. Even so, that night everything looked and sounded strange. My footsteps echoed in the hush of the room. In the back recesses, flickering red lights looked like the eyes of night creatures, even though I knew they were just the "on" lights of amps. All around us, long black coils of cords snaked in the shadows, hugging the walls where it was darkest.

I was cold. I rubbed my arms and stared into the vocal booth in the far right corner. In it, a tall boom with a mike dangling off the end stood framed by the booth's window. It looked like a hangman's gallows, the mike like a choked head.

Suddenly my chest started shaking. A wave of loneliness washed over me. In that moment, I understood the human urge to invent heavens and teachings of reincarnation. I needed the impossible—to see Sam again. I walked away from the girls, fighting to get a mental grip.

An arm wrapped around my shoulders and gave me a hug. Luanne touched her head to mine and said, "We're done. You need me to drive you home?"

"Nah. I'm fine. Thanks," I said and left without saying good-bye.

I drove all the way across town, but once at my condo I drove on by. I didn't think about where I was going. The car took I-440 West toward Memphis and headed down the 46th Street exit ramp toward Sam's.

I took a right on Charlotte and drove slowly past the pawn shop. There was nothing to see really, just some lights left on in the back. I kept going and took a left at 51st Avenue by St. Ann's Church and went into Sylvan Park, Uncle Ralph's neighborhood.

His car and truck were both in the driveway. The house was dark as I expected—it was already after ten o'clock. But as I passed, I saw a movement on the porch. Uncle Ralph recognized my car and got up from his glider, raising his hand as he came down the steps.

"Hey, sweetheart," he said. "I've been thinking about you." His hands rested in my window as he bent down to see me. "You making it all right?"

I nodded. "You're up late tonight."

"Aw, I don't sleep much." I noticed his face seemed thinner. The age spots around his hairline stood out more against his pale skin.

"I'm just wandering," I said. "I worked tonight and didn't feel like going home yet. You'll probably think I'm weird, but I thought I might go over to Sam's place." I shrugged as I looked at him, not knowing how to explain my feelings.

"Sure," he said. "Let me tell Lucille and I'll go with you."

Ralph walked ahead of me up the stairs. He pulled away some of the yellow barrier tape still hanging on the sides of the door.

"I haven't been back up here since . . . lately. The cops never told me if they were through or not. I figure they're done." He unlocked the office door with his key and switched on the hanging overhead light.

I ran my hand along the top of the client chair as Ralph opened the apartment door. While his steps echoed on the wooden floors, I sat down at the desk, laid my head on it, and reached my arms out across it as far as they would go.

Ralph raised a few windows. Before long a breeze made its way through the rooms. I walked into the apartment without the apprehension I'd experienced while the police were there. It was like home again. The single lamp Ralph turned on cast a soothing light over the bookshelves and my favorite chair—the overstuffed green one with an ottoman—beside them.

I closed my eyes thinking how odd it was to feel so lonely and disoriented earlier at Ju-Ju's, a place I'd worked a hundred times, and to feel such relief here so close to the scene of a murder.

"Was there something you needed to get while you're here?" Ralph asked.

Before I could say anything, the phone rang.

I rubbed my head. "I should have come back over and done some work before now, Ralph. I'm sorry, I wasn't thinking. His clients are probably wondering about the status of their cases."

I got up and turned off the answering machine before

picking up the receiver.

"Hello?"

There was a coarse intake of breath. A man cleared his throat, a loud and lengthy process, then in a voice that was a cross between a frog and a demon from hell said, "You must be Willi."

"That's right. Who's this?"

The caller responded with a coughing fit and another drawn-out throat clearing. He didn't answer my question but grunged out "I knew you'd come back."

His voice scared me. Uncle Ralph could tell and came over to me. "Crank call?" he asked.

I shrugged. "Who is this?" I asked again.

On the other end of the line, the voice said "S-h-am."

*This guy is plastered*, I thought. Drunk or not, I didn't appreciate his saying he was Sam.

"That's not funny," I said, looking over to the caller ID screen for his phone number.

"It'sh not on there," he said.

"Can you see me?" I asked. I picked up the phone and walked to the window overlooking The Club Car, the little beer joint next door. It was too far down. Next to it, the tattoo parlor had a second story but was still too low for anyone to see in Sam's windows.

"Coursh not," he said. "Why I called. *Want* to sh-h-ee you."

I didn't like this a bit. "Listen, bud. I don't know who you are, or what you want with me, but I'm not in the mood to be your A.A. partner."

I was about to hang up on him when I heard "Wait, wait!" Putting the receiver back to my ear, I listened to him cough again.

"You're right," he said. "Had too many. Call me tomorrow. 555-1259. Tell you where we can meet. About S-h-am."

"Wait," I said, writing down the number. "I don't even—"

Click. I shook the receiver then listened again like a dummy, as if shaking it would reconnect us.

Ralph stood in the doorway with a questioning look on his

face. I hung up, looking out the window again. In the street below us, a big guy on a motorcycle idled slowly past our building. He gunned his motor and shot out of sight.

*About Sam.* Did he mean about his being killed? Probably not. More likely it was just an old friend or a client. I ripped the number off the pad and told Ralph, "I think I'm ready to go now."

I slept fitfully that night. I tossed and flipped so much that Buddy, who usually never complains about anything, huffed, moaned, and finally jumped off the bed to sleep on the rug.

I awoke with a start at 4:45 A.M. feeling my chest for bullet holes. My arms and legs were so tensed up, they were starting to cramp. I got up to shake them out. Knowing I'd never get back to sleep, I went to the kitchen.

With a glass of milk and a bag of butter cookies, I got comfortable on the living room couch and channel surfed through early-morning news shows, infomercials, and bad cinema.

I decided on a Stupid Woman movie. You know the type: if there's a chase scene, she trips because she's running uphill on rugged terrain in high heels; or if her husband/lover beats the crap out of her, she goes back so he can keep doing it; or she's been threatened or stalked, and she slips away from her police protection to go buy panty hose.

"Don't go in there!" I said to the screen as the female lead entered a dark parking garage. Buddy snuggled up beside me and woofed to her in agreement. I gave him a cookie.

"Stupid Woman!" I said. "Can't you hear the scary music?"

She obviously couldn't and entered the building. I checked her shoes. Six-inch heels.

Buddy woofed again and smiled. I knew he was just sucking up to get another cookie. Still, it's nice to have somebody listen to you and go along with whatever you say. I gave him another one.

*These movies are so predictable,* I thought. A woman gets

a phone call from a mysterious stranger and agrees to meet him on his own turf, knowing that one murder has already been committed, probably someone she knew.

As the music crescendoed, a knife flashed in the dimly lit garage.

"Stupid Wo—"

I stopped and held my breath. Buddy finished with a "Wo, wo, wo" then licked his chops in anticipation.

I felt like I'd been hit over the head with a two-by-four. After forty years of cynical finger pointing, it was quite a shock to realize that I was, in fact, The Stupid Damn Woman. How could I have even considered going off to meet that drunk who'd called? I hadn't been thinking clearly at Sam's office. Whatever this guy had to say, he could forget it.

Time to get my act together. I had an important session scheduled the next day. I decided to go to Sam's beforehand and send out final bills for his clients. Then I'd listen to the Guiness tapes. If anything struck me as relevant, I'd call Detective Bracken and act like I'd just found Sam's stash.

# CHAPTER 7

"MIND IF I SEE THE REST OF THE PLACE?" Jill came by Sam's office to pick me up the next day. We had a session with Jud Sherrill, the record producer who'd given us our first big break in Nashville twenty years earlier.

I unlocked the connecting door to the apartment. It was musty in there, so I opened windows as she inspected.

"Not bad," she said. "It's cool in a low-class, funky kind of way."

For some reason, I took offense at this remark. "I love it," I said. "It reminds me of that first apartment Luanne and I had in Sheffield."

Jill snapped her fingers. "Exactly. It's got the same high ceilings and old hardwood floors. And the same ugly kitchen," she said. I heard the curtain swish on the one odd-sized window. "What a horrible view." The junkyard mutt across the alley woofed at her from his fenced empire of tall grass and rusty car parts.

She peeked down the hall at the bedroom and bathroom. Her smile couldn't hide the slightly disapproving look on her face.

"It's not *that* bad," I said.

Looking out the front windows, she said, "At least I don't have bums and crazy people walking the streets in my neighborhood. I hope you aren't going in and out of here at night."

I looked across Charlotte Avenue to the bus stop. A man with tattoos on his forearms walked in front of the park. His skin was that color of red that men get from working outside all their lives. A cigarette hung loosely from his mouth as he switched a six-pack to the other arm.

He ignored an old woman as she passed. She was a regular; every time I saw her, she was talking to herself as she made her rounds, wandering the same route every day. She crossed at the red light, coming toward Sam's building.

Once Sam introduced her to me. She loved him. He would stand there and nod while she talked crazy. After a while, he'd laugh at something she said, or catch her eyes and smile way down into them. For a minute, that would bring her into the *now* enough to make her seem almost normal.

He always gave her something, whatever he had on him, like a button or some trinket found in the street. She didn't care what he gave her. Anything pleased her. She'd take the gift, put it in her raincoat pocket, and smile like a schoolgirl before moving down the block.

"Give me some gum," I said to Jill. She always carried a huge purse of the Let's-Make-A-Deal variety with one of everything in there. If I asked for a hand grenade, she'd probably rummage around and fish one out.

"I'll be right back." I ran out the door and down the stairs. When I saw the old lady looking in the pawn shop, I realized she'd never actually spoken to me before. She was talking louder than usual.

I cleared my throat. "Hey," I said and lamely wiggled my fingers at her.

She brushed her gauzy blue scarf back a little. Barely turning toward me, she peered out thick black cat-eye glasses, still talking but more quietly.

I smiled and tried again. "Hey, Macie. I'm Willi, remember? Sam's friend." I hitched my thumb up toward the office.

She pulled her raincoat closer around her. For a moment, I thought she didn't understand me. Behind the lenses, the dark magnified spots of her eyes moved up and down. She wiped a blotched hand across her lips.

"Sam's my boyfriend," she told me flatly. "He brings me presents. He gave me this." She brought up a brown wallet from her purse. "And this," she said, showing me a little teddy bear with one arm. She unzipped a pouch and let me see the corner of a white lace handkerchief before carefully tucking it back in. "I'm saving this for Buckingham Palace."

"Good idea," I said, doing my best to imitate Sam. I held out the pack of gum. "Want some?"

She shook her head. "Rots your teeth. Dr. Krantz don't want me chewing it, but my lawyer says I can do what I want to, and he'll help me. He gave me this," she said, holding up a pen, "and this," holding up fingernail clippers. I put the gum back in my jacket pocket.

I wondered if she knew about Sam. I didn't want to cause her unnecessary pain but felt since she was his friend, she should know.

Suddenly Macie lost her balance and fell into me. I gripped her bone-thin arm and held on until she felt steady.

"I'm fine," she said. "My legs give out sometimes."

"Macie," I said as I let go, "Sam's dead."

She stood still for a long while. "I seen the police," she said finally. "They looked at me. A big man come over and asked me questions—did I see anything unusual, where was I this, when was I that?

"Said he was the boss and showed me a badge. Looked fake to me. I told my lawyer and he said they could not ask me no more questions without the presents to my attorney. And I'd have told that to the police but they never asked me no more questions. But they kept looking at me. They looked at me and looked at me."

Her lower lip trembled. Her eyes glazed over as she turned toward Richland Park, where children ran toward the swings, laughing and squealing. Macie's face muscles relaxed into a childlike expression of its own, like she was caught up in an old memory.

I couldn't understand her mumbling. She shuffled off without a good-bye, her mouth moving in another secret conversation. She pulled the blue gauze closer around her face and neck, stepping back into the comfort of her daydream world.

"Are you ready?" I said, opening the office door.

"Yeah," Jill said. "We ought to get going. I told Luanne I'd pick her up. You got any of that gum left?"

"Yeah, she didn't want it." I felt in my right pocket, then the left.

"Well, where is it?"

I reached into my jeans pockets, although I knew I hadn't put the gum there. I patted my jacket again. Nothing.

"Maybe you dropped it on the stairs. We can look as we leave," Jill said.

I pulled the door closed and locked it. On the way out, we looked but didn't find the pack.

"You're losing it, Willi. You must have given it to her."

As we stood on the sidewalk, I pictured Macie as she fell into me.

*That little sneak.* I closed my eyes and started laughing, imagining her opening her purse and saying to the next patsy, "She gave me this," while she reaches in and pulls out a pack of gum.

MetroMedia Entertainment, Inc. sprawled over twenty acres along the Cumberland River. Jud Sherrill built his complex with minimal destruction to the wooded area he'd bought for his father many years ago. Although surrounded by industrial parks and very close to downtown Nashville, the buildings were tucked neatly away in the trees. Only an occasional flash of color from the interstate exchange a few miles away reminded me we weren't in the country.

On either side of the road, I could see wooden signs next to nature trails pointing the way to various buildings as we drove in. Through the trees, a few park benches were visible in clearings and flower gardens.

We parked in front of the main building, which housed three recording studios—one large room for cutting tracks and two smaller ones for overdubs and mixing. We would be working in Studio B, one of the small ones.

When we stepped inside, the three of us said "Wow" at the same time. Rather than the cold atmosphere of most reception areas, the room had the feel of a cozy front porch. At the far end, we could see the floor-to-ceiling glass open out to a back veranda that overlooked the river.

We followed the curve of the room to a wide hallway that drew us in. Deep mahogany paneling covered the walls all the way up to the twenty-foot ceiling. It looked like an art gallery with individual lights over huge black-and-white photograph enlargements. Spaced down the length of the hall, they ended at a foyer with passageways to each studio.

The photos were in chronological order, a story in pictures of Jud Sherrill's amazing career. Two taken the same night were grouped together at the entrance. The first showed him as a tall, skinny kid on stage at the Grand Ole Opry, playing an upright bass. The second was a close-up of him, only fourteen years old, his hair slicked back and his face shining with the innocence of farms. His father smiled into the camera, too, as it captured his proudest moment, when the dream that his boy would play the Ryman came true.

We walked down the time line, passing each phase of musical change from the fifties to present with the corresponding fashions in clothes and hairstyles. In each, Jud posed with celebrities of country music as well as stars from TV and films.

"Look," Jill said, "we're in this one." Luanne and I caught up with her down the hall.

The group shot had been taken the night of our first session for Jud, the one where Luanne "stripped." At the time, the reason for the picture was a drop-by visit from Web Foley, one in a long line of flamboyant mayors in Nashville's history. But the value of this photo now was not due to the harmonica-playing former politician; it was the diminutive seventeen-year-old girl at the center.

Jennalyn Wade, scared to death and still a brunette, smiled gamely into the camera. The spark of ambition in her eyes that night was the only physical characteristic she retained of her former self. Now blonde and professionally sculpted, Jennalyn became an internationally known model and film star. Getting her start in country music, then crossing over to the pop market, her chiseled features made her memorable to millions of fans and a natural for cosmetics ad campaigns.

This first album did more than make her an overnight success—it also boosted Jud's production career to a higher level. The stunning debut showcased Jud's talent for choosing the right songs. His unique visions in arrangements perfectly highlighted Jen's abilities.

It hadn't hurt us either. Of course, our part was small. But Jud outdid himself that night, guiding us through intricate harmonies that made us sound like a band of country angels. Although we had worked on many records before then, that one increased our bookings in Nashville enough to justify moving here.

"Who are these little geeks?" Luanne said. Her black hair shone under the picture's light. She reached into the inside pocket of her red blazer and put on her glasses.

Three young boys stood on the outside of the group. "That's Rick Crawford," I said, "without all the hair." He must have been at least twenty, although he didn't look it.

"Look here at Jud's son, Blaine," Jill said. "They were all gofers then. Blaine and his buddy here, can't remember his name, were in high school together, I remember that. They worked during summer break."

"I wonder what made Rick come here," I said.

Jill shook her head. "Don't know," she said and started waving her arms toward the end of the hall. "Come on, y'all. Let's get going."

"Yes, Mama," Luanne said and followed.

Something held me at the picture. I stared into the faces—Jennalyn's trademark dimples, Jud's eyes squinting together in a laugh, Web Foley's comic profile as he slapped Jud on the back, a harmonica dangling at his side.

We were young, and at the time, I couldn't imagine a day when I'd forget the least detail of such an important event. But looking from this end of twenty years, I hardly remembered even myself, what I had been like.

"Move it, Willi," Jill said from the doorway. "If we're late, Jud may not call us for another year."

With a vague sense that something was wrong, I pulled away. As I walked, it felt like the picture followed me. Even the sounds from that night seemed to drag behind me like the tin crackling of a shortwave radio, its static interfering in and out of half-conversations, string passages, inverted laughter.

I looked back from the end foyer down the quiet hall. Nothing had changed. No eyes moved in the photo. No smoky figures floated out to say "Boo!" I sighed, attributing the odd feeling to the simplest explanation—I had seen a ghost. My own.

I padded down the low-pile carpet to the doors of Studio B. Next to the lintel, a big wall sconce lit up. Its red glow told us a recording was in progress inside, so we waited.

"You know, it sure was easy to get in here," Luanne said. "No receptionist or secretary up front. You'd think they'd have better security in a place like this."

I put my hands on Luanne's shoulders and gently walked her up against the wall. I put my finger alongside her cheek, pointed up to a tiny lens aimed at the studio door, and said, "Big Brother, little sister. Don't pick your nose." Luanne self-consciously lowered her hand from her face.

"They're all over the building," I said. "I wouldn't be surprised if they were camouflaged in birds' nests outside."

The red light went out. I pulled with all my strength on the heavy door, which opened into a buffer. The overhead light blinded us a moment before we entered the dark interior of the control room.

It was blue. Recessed into the ceiling, blue gels shone on the mixing board. Its surface, also blue, reflected the color back up, which gave the room an otherworldly glow.

The engineer was a stranger, so I assumed he was from somewhere else. He turned his head, waved, and went back to work. On the other side of him, an oversized chair rolled into our view. It creaked as its occupant stood and came toward us with outstretched arms.

Jud's voice boomed a drawn-out "*Where* in the *hell* have y'all *been*?" in a funny exaggerated accent.

Jill put her arms around him. "Us? Where have *you* been?"

"Rightcheer," he said and gave me and Luanne each a hug. "Hey, how did y'all like your picture out there? I saw you gawking at it."

He ushered us to the end of the mixing console. Under a glass top, four small video screens tilted up. Jud slid a hand-sized panel open, revealing controls for the screens. Like a kid showing off a new toy, he demonstrated the different views he could call up—front and back doors, halls, and even the other control rooms.

"Pretty nifty, huh?" he said. As he switched back to the main hall, someone with long curly hair walked past the photo gallery. It was the only movement on any screen.

We settled down and listened to the one song we would be working on. The session went smoothly, as they always do with Jud. He knew what he wanted and exactly where our parts would fall.

"That's great, ladies," he said. "If y'all want a copy, we'll fix you up with a rough mix right quick."

"Is it okay if we look around a little bit?" Jill asked.

"Sure," he said. "Make yourself at home. There's coffee and cappuccino straight down that hall to your right."

I fumbled around in my purse for a cigarette. Even though the work had been simple, I was getting edgy.

"Is there a quick way outside from here?" I asked.

With her arms folded across her chest, Jill said, "I thought you quit."

"Quit what?" I said. "Breathing? I just need a little fresh air." I closed my purse and stood.

"Go in the studio and through that side door," Jud said. "I've got a nice little rose garden out there."

The girls went for the coffee. I went out. Jud was right—the garden was small but laid out beautifully. I sat on the park bench in the center and lit up.

I'd smoked about half my cigarette when I heard a twig snap in the woods to my right. It was a loud break, as if something heavy had stepped on it. I glanced in that direction but didn't see anything. I went back to staring at a large rose bloom close by and, on impulse, reached out and down to touch it.

I felt something zing over me like a puff of wind at the top of my hair. Not ten feet from me, the trunk of a little dogwood tree splintered. One of its low branches smashed down into a red rose bush, causing its petals to fall like drops of blood. I screamed and hit the ground.

I threw my body under the park bench. Being cramped in such a tiny space, my chin against my chest, my heartbeat sounded like a jackhammer.

I held my breath and listened. Nothing. I tried to shift my weight. I couldn't turn my neck, so my view was limited to the half-circle of roses between me and the studio.

My ankles started quivering. I waited, listening for what seemed like hours. Still there was no sound or movement around me. No one ran away. No one ran to my rescue after hearing me scream.

*Didn't I scream?* It felt like my brain was doing backflips. While I tried to get a grip, the pain in my right knee worsened by the second. I knew I couldn't last under there much longer. Bullet or no bullet, I had to move.

On the other side of the roses, I heard the outside studio door open. Footsteps came toward me on the mulch path. They stopped at the edge of the garden for a moment, then shuffled inside the circle of roses. With my legs cramping and my eyes tightly closed, I willed myself invisible.

It didn't work.

"What are you doing down there?"

A mixture of relief and dread came over me as I slid out. It was Jill with Luanne right behind her.

"Get down!" I said. At least that's what I tried to say. Air moved through my mouth, but nothing intelligible came out. The look on my face did make them get down. Not to take shelter—to grab me and pull me up.

"No! No!" I said, fighting them, but they sat me down on the bench anyway. I wrestled out of their hands and jumped up to scan the woods around us.

"What is wrong with you?" Luanne said.

I looked in every direction. Other than a few chipmunks, we were completely alone. With a thump, I sat down between the girls and hid my face in my hands. My body started shaking. It was hard to breathe.

"Someone shot at me," I gasped finally. I got up again to look around, then turned to my friends—who laughed—both of them. While they chuckled, they did look around a little bit, but not anxiously, not as if they believed me.

I looked from one to the other—at Jill's eyebrows starting to scrunch down and at Luanne still laughing.

"There's nobody out there, you dumbass," Luanne said. She slapped Jill on the arm and said, "Maybe it's time to tell her about your friend."

Jill didn't move or answer. A solemn look replaced her smile as her brows furrowed into a deep V.

"You know," Luanne said, "your *friend*, the psy—"

"Hush," Jill said, never taking her eyes off me. In all the time I'd known her, it was a look I'd never seen before. I couldn't read it and that scared me.

I sat down again. "What are you talking about?"

Jill took my hands in hers and squeezed. "Willi, I have a friend," she said gently, "who is a doctor. She's a good listener. I've mentioned you to her, about how you've had a rough time lately—"

"What?" I yelled. "Are we talking about a shrink? What do you mean, you've told her about me?"

"It's nothing to be ashamed of," Jill said.

"Believe me," I said, "shame is not even close to what I'm feeling right now." My jaw was clenched so tight it barely moved as I spoke.

"I knew she'd get mad," Luanne said.

"She's hard-headed as a mule. Look, Willi—"

"No, *you* look. Read my lips," I said and began a slow, emphatic series of charades. "Somebody. SHOT. At. Me." My hands fired and released a make-believe gun. Wiggling my fingers as if signing, I said, "I. Don't. Need. No. Damn. Psychiatrist."

Luanne looked stunned. She blinked her big brown eyes

and nodded with what I took as comprehension until she said, "Cussing *and* using double negatives. By George, she's mad all right."

Running my fingers into my hair and clutching my scalp, I growled and twirled around. When I stopped, I looked down. Some of the rose petals were at my feet. I started to grin.

"Y'all are going to feel so stupid when you see this," I said and walked over to the dogwood. "This branch didn't break off by itself. What about this bullet hole right here in this tree?"

But as I knelt and pointed, I couldn't find one. I began patting the ground all around the tree, feeling nothing but leaves and dirt. I pivoted to the right to check the branch. No hole. I searched the entire area around it and the tree again. No bullet.

I stood up and brushed off my hands, knees, and the front of my dress. The girls said nothing.

"I am not making this up," I said.

"Would you just calm down and listen to me for a second?" Jill said. "I'm not saying nothing happened. Obviously something scared you. But if we think about it, I bet things can be explained some other way."

"Like how?"

"Well, the shot, for instance. Couldn't that have been from the barge company or the rock crusher place down there?"

As luck would have it, a loud crash sounded just then from down the river.

"See?" Jill said. "Sounds like construction blasting. Dynamite. The railroad bridge isn't far away, either. When they're doing repairs on those lines it's awful noisy."

"But it wasn't like that," I said. "I *felt* it go over my head."

Luanne had been standing behind Jill. She took a step to the side to peep around at me before speaking up.

"Maybe a bird flew over you right when the dynamite or whatever blasted, and then it landed in the tree and the limb broke off."

Jill and I looked at each other. "A *bird* did that?" I asked, jerking my head toward the branch.

Luanne shrugged and said, "A very fat bird?"

I could feel my hands trembling as I stuffed them in my jacket pocket. I closed my eyes to concentrate. What did the shot sound like? Could it have been something else? I wasn't exactly an expert on how a gun would sound on the receiving end.

The beginnings of a tension headache throbbed in my neck. While I rubbed it, I tried to see things from my friends' point of view—that I was nuts.

I couldn't take the way they stared at me. The mixture of pity and disbelief was unbearable, so I turned back to the dogwood. I dropped to my knees again to sweep the ground one more time. They whispered behind me, but at that point I didn't even try to hear what they said.

After a few minutes of searching, I'd found nothing. I got up and walked around the edge of the clearing, looking deep into the trees. "I can't understand why you don't believe me," I said to the woods. "You would rather make up some way-out fantasy than listen to me. Why?"

"Willi, saying somebody shot at you is pretty way-out. Can't you see that yet?" Jill took a few steps in my direction. I walked further around the circle away from her. Her voice took on a pleading note. "There was no one out here but you. Did you hear someone run away?"

I shook my head.

"Luanne, when we came out to get Willi, did you hear anything? See anyone?"

"No," she replied.

"Neither did I," Jill said, "and we would have, since we were looking for you. How long were you under that bench?"

"Not long," I said. "A few minutes maybe."

"Long enough to shoot again? Why didn't he?"

"Maybe it was a drive-by shooting," Luanne said.

Jill and I gave her hard looks like we always do when she says something stupid, a fairly frequent occurrence.

"We're in the woods, Luanne. There's no road to drive by on," I said. "You two go back inside. I'll catch up with you in a minute."

Another boom from downriver made Jill point toward it. Before she could say "See?" I said, "Go. I'll be right there."

"What are you fixing to do?" Jill asked.

"Look around a little more."

"Don't be mad," Luanne said. "Come in with us. Just to be safe."

"Safe from what? Being dive-bombed by a big fat swooping bird? I'm nuts, remember? There's absolutely nothing to be afraid of, according to y'all."

I didn't want to be angry with my friends. I didn't want to be around them either. Although I was out of patience, I tried to put a little tenderness into my voice.

"Please. Go on in. I need to think a minute."

I stepped into the woods, walking slowly. I guess I was hoping a bent twig or a torn piece of clothing caught in a bush would jump out at me like what happens in the movies. I was not so lucky.

I didn't watch Luanne and Jill walk away, but when I heard the studio door click shut I turned toward the building.

Behind me, I lined up the empty bench with the broken limb. And before me, on the other side of trees from which the shot must have come, was a stretch of possibilities I didn't want to consider.

The studio. Small balconies on each of four levels faced the river. At the top, a long canvas covered a larger balcony. Adjacent to it was an open area with yellow table umbrellas and lounge chairs for sunbathing.

And on ground level, the back veranda was wide open. The railing curved around the width of the building with steps down to the parking lot on each side.

I didn't want to hear what I was telling myself. *You heard no one run away through the woods because no one was in the woods. The shot came from in the studio.*

As frightening as it was to think someone shot at me— someone I must know—the alternative was not much better: *You heard no one run away because you imagined the whole thing.*

Whichever was true, I was red-hot. Every aspect infuriated me—that someone shot at me; that the shooter was likely someone I know; that my best friends not only don't believe me, but think I'm crazy; that they've already discussed my insanity behind my back with a complete stranger who, by the way, treats the mentally unbalanced; and that I might *be* mentally unbalanced.

"God help them all if I'm not," I said out loud as I stomped toward the building to look for a guilty face.

A cool breeze hit me as I looked out from the veranda. The wooden planks creaked as I paced from one side to the other looking for something, a spent shell, anything.

I found nothing unusual. At each end I held to the railings while stepping down slowly, looking underneath, and searching the ground for footprints to the parking lot. No luck there either. Large stepping stones spaced from the porch to the lot didn't have enough ground between them for as much as a baby shoe's imprint. I walked the length again, going behind the row of rocking chairs and, finally, back inside to a blast of air-conditioning.

In the lounge/waiting room, no one lounged or waited. I strolled a circular path around the quiet room, then headed for the main hallway.

When I walked past the photo gallery, I remembered Jud said he'd seen us on his monitor in the studio. I glanced back self-consciously, then up in the ceiling crevices of the foyer, wondering if someone watched me.

An arrow pointed straight ahead to Studio A. Entering the dimly lit hallway, I breathed in the smell of new wood and electronics. The gray carpet muted my steps as I passed through light then shadows cast by widely spaced sconces high on the wall. I walked past the studio door to find the balcony.

It was outside a break room where two girls sat in a booth. Another dropped coins in a soft-drink machine. The outside sliding-glass door was partially open. Through it, I could see a guy smoking on the balcony. I slid the door open wider and stood on the threshold.

"Excuse me. Did you hear anything unusual about five or ten minutes ago?"

"We just came out of the studio," the guy said.

"It would have been like a big boom or crack." I didn't want to say "like a gunshot" or anything that might scare them unnecessarily. The girls shook their heads.

"Ah, well. It's no big deal," I said, sticking my head further out the door. I looked around the balcony floor. Nothing there, only about fifty cigarette butts. "Thanks anyway."

As I walked back the way I came, bass notes thumped like mortars behind the wall on my right. Further on, the *chink-chink* of a rhythm guitar sliced through. *Good*, I thought. *Should be lots of friends in there. And maybe one enemy.* I yanked the door open anyway and went on in.

Studio A was considerably bigger than B, where we had just worked. The control rooms were about the same, but the recording floor was three or four times larger. A full grand piano took up most of the studio's left side.

Spanning the back wall were three isolation booths, little rooms that muffle loud instruments. The booth behind the piano looked set up for a vocalist. The middle one was stuffed with the drums, cymbals, and various other percussion instruments of a full kit. In a chair in front of the right booth sat Gary Phillips, a silver-haired studio veteran, holding his guitar. His cord ran behind him, under the booth's door, and into his amp.

Seated by the right wall, the bass player sipped coffee. Between him and the extra-long end of the piano, three flattened music stands surrounded a padded stool. The stands overflowed with charts and notebooks. On top of them sat a miniature boom box and a cup with brown drip stains down the sides. All the musicians watched the man who commanded from the center of the room, Jud Sherrill's partner for many years, Harrell Gentry.

While I took all this in, I stood quietly in the back of the control room. The engineer finished twiddling with knobs and turned his head slowly toward me. He had a mean look on his face that would've scared the pants off someone who didn't know him.

"Grrrrr," I said to Jeff Jernigan, a well-known Nashville engineer, and returned his scowl.

The lines on Jeff's face turned up as he stretched his arms out. I bent down to his neck and nuzzled the soft fur of his beard. He gave me a kiss and said, "Where's the rest of the Harem?"

"In B." All the questions I'd intended to ask seemed stupid as I hugged Jeff and looked out at my friends. They were in the middle of a session, for goodness' sake. They didn't have time to kill me. Besides, it would be mighty hard to walk across the studio floor carrying a weapon.

Or would it? Next to each musician was at least one bag for carrying gear. Gary had two by his chair for his cords and accessories, plus two guitar cases. He could have had two or three handguns and a couple of assault rifles in there and no one would know it. Even Harrell, the producer, had a soft-side leather briefcase beside his stool.

"What is it?" Jeff asked.

"Nothing," I said. "Just wanted to say 'hi.' What time did y'all start today?"

"Twelve. We'll probably break after we get this cut."

Nobody walked out during takes. I knew one thing for certain—none of these guys could have been the shooter.

From the floor, Harrell wrapped up his orders to the troops. He turned sideways toward us and said, "Let's take one. You ready in there, J. J.?"

Jeff nodded. He punched the red button on his remote, setting the big recorder in motion. Holding down another button on the console, he said, "We're rolling," into everyone's headsets.

"I'm outta here, babe," I said. "See you."

He winked and blew me a kiss as drumsticks clacked the count off. I returned to the hallway, passing the red light that signaled track-in-progress. With a shudder I realized it could also signal danger.

On the way to Studio B, I found myself hoping Jill and

Luanne had already gone to the car. I went straight to the break room on that floor. Sweeping the curtain aside, I found the balcony's sliding-glass door locked. I fiddled with the latch a while but, seeing only a few leaves on the balcony anyway, gave up.

I walked slowly toward the control room of B, trying to talk myself out of going in. I already knew who had been in there before the shot. I'd just met the engineer, and Jud was beyond suspicion, so why bother? It would be a waste of time when I could be checking out the rest of the building. Plus I wasn't ready to see the girls yet.

My luck ran true to form. Just as I passed the door, it opened. Jill leaned against it, and with the inner door propped open, I had a clear view of the console. The engineer sat alone at the board.

"Where's Jud?" I asked.

"He went to make a few calls. In his office," the engineer said.

I nodded and turned to walk away.

"Not so fast. Where are you going?" Jill asked.

"Just looking around," I said.

"Willi, please don't go around talking . . . being . . . ."

"Say it. Go on, let it out."

"I *told* you I don't think you're crazy," she said in an exasperated tone. She flipped her hair back on both sides and crossed her arms over her chest. "I just think whatever happened is mixed up in your head, that's all."

"That's the definition of *crazy*," I said while feeling around in the bottom of my purse. I really didn't care for her opinion and considered telling her so. Instead, I pulled out a cigarette and stuck it on my lip.

Jill didn't approve. "They probably don't want you smoking in here," she said.

I bit the filter and smiled at her like The Joker. Walking closer to the door, I looked up to the lens mounted at the top of the frame. I held the lighter up to it, clicked purposefully, and lit up anyway.

"You know what?" I said, blowing smoke up to the camera. "I don't really give a diddly-damn."

Miss Priss hated it when I cussed, but she knew better than to correct me right then. We stared at each other a while. I smoked. She fumed.

"Besides," I said, "there's no such thing as a non-smoking studio." I didn't bring up the fact that the only smoker I'd seen so far was technically out of the building.

Her arms tightened across her chest. She took a breath to speak, but I cut in before she had a chance. "Are our tapes ready yet?"

"Not yet."

"All I'm doing is looking around, okay? I am not running around acting the fool or anything like that."

"I'm just worried about you," she said, trying to sound sweet but failing.

"No." I pointed at her with the two fingers holding my cigarette. "Not about me. You're worried I'm going to rock the boat. That I'll say something that might hurt our chances of being hired here again." I stared at her a long while, my cigarette in the air as I considered crossing the line. The conversation on the other side was one I'd stopped short of many, many times. I was too upset and angry to do so now.

"You're worried I'm gonna quit playing the game," I said. "Aren't you tired of it? Look how this business has changed us, Jill. We're hardly even friends anymore. We're not even nice anymore."

"Speak for yourself," she said.

"All I'm saying is we've done our time. For the past twenty years, we've bent over backwards to look and act the way these boys want. But has it done us any good? No, we *still* have to look and act like brain-dead Miss Americas, put up with ungodly sexist insults and superior male—"

"What are you raving about? None of that is true! Calm down and lower your voice," Jill hissed through gritted teeth.

"*And*," I said louder, "we've got to always be *calm*, and lower our voices, and play like everything is just fine. Well, I've done that. Over and over again. But I draw the line when bullets start flying over my head. Maybe *you* can pretend it never happened, but I can't."

I took a long drag and noticed my left foot was tapping furiously. Jill put her hands up in the air and said, "Fine. Whatever you say. I'm not going to argue with you when you're like this."

"Fine," I said and headed off for Studio C.

I think my little outburst was a sign of shock wearing off. Not that I intended to apologize to Jill. I didn't. I meant what I said.

We *had* changed. It seemed the more I pulled to the left— *left* being that place assigned to us non-conservative women by WASPs like Jill—the more of a hard right mind-set *she* adopted. We never talked about it, but we had become very different people. Today's outburst was inevitable and a long time in coming.

I'm sure she'd call that overreacting. Maybe it was. Out of the blue, her husband's truck came to mind, a big red Dodge with gun racks and NRA stickers. I yanked the heavy door to Studio C open so hard I almost hit the wall behind it.

"Wait! Could you hold that door for me?" A young woman came out of the break room holding three coffees. She scurried toward me, keeping her eyes on the cups.

"Thanks," she said when I grabbed the interior door too. Stepping inside, I took a quick look through the glass. A single vocal mike stood in the middle of the floor.

The coffee girl set the cups down in front of Rick Crawford at the producer's table. He picked up a packet of sweetener by the corner and shook it while swiveling around to me. His long locks of curly brown hair were tossed aside with one flick of the neck. He shot out a smug look intended to send greenhorns running back out the door.

Undaunted, I shot a strong one of my own at him and enjoyed watching his attitude disintegrate, even if it only lasted a moment.

I felt the tug of Scots-Irish ancestors in my blood, already revved up from my little chat with Jill. It's not that I *wanted* to fight. It's not my fault there is a deep, natural, centuries-old enmity between the self-righteous control freaks of the world and the scruffy ranks they would enslave. Namely me.

In other words, he brought out the white trash in me. I took a deep breath. As much as he irritated me, I was determined to remain calm.

We ping-ponged the usual small talk until finally he said, "I didn't know you were going to be here today."

*So what*, I thought. Why should he? Since when was he privy to Jud's scheduling? And why did it sound like he was lying?

"Well, I am," I said. I smiled like Scarlett flirting with Ashley. "You know, I was wondering . . . um . . . could I ask you a question?"

"You just did," he said, his mouth revealing shark teeth that were too straight and too white.

"Ha—HAH! You witty Californians." I fake-laughed and patted the top of his hand a few times, willing myself not to grab his fingers and pull them backwards. "No, really. I just wanted to ask your *permission* . . . ?" I said in the voice of my aunt Ruby, who ends every sentence going up a few notes into a question. ". . . to look *around? I've* lost my *lighter somewhere? And* can't *find it?*"

"Sure," he said. "Cheryl, have you seen a lighter?"

The coffee girl was cleaning the heads of a two-track recorder behind us. "No," she said and returned to work.

I felt behind couch cushions and pretended to look all over the control room. I continued searching out on the studio floor, concentrating around the standing mike under the light.

Behind the glass windows, I could see Rick grab the telephone on the producer's table. He shouldered the receiver and said something to Cheryl. It must have been a question. At first, she started to shake her head. Then glancing in my direction, she shrugged her shoulders and said, "Maybe."

*Time to go*, I thought. I was sure he'd asked her if I had been in there earlier.

"Can y'all hear me?" My words sounded hollow in the acoustically dead room.

The giant speakers in the wall clicked on as Rick said, "Yes, ma'am," in a mock Southern accent.

*Jerk*, I thought. "I don't see it out here. Sorry to bother you." I waved and exited quickly out the side door into the hallway.

When Jill saw me come out of the building, she pulled her car up to the sidewalk.

"You okay?" she and Luanne said at the same time.

They didn't talk as we drove away from the complex through the woods. Neither did I. I was too busy worrying about the black Honda with a dent in the grill that followed us out of the parking lot.

I had seen it before. I just couldn't remember where.

# CHAPTER 8

THE AFTERNOON SUN came in Sam's office windows at a low slant. In the street below, rush hour was in full swing on Charlotte. The road noise of engines mixed with radios, blaring that special Nashville blend—country, easy listening, and head-banger rock. First one took the lead, then another, then all three would rise together at top volume like a discordant jazz trio, each on his own trip.

I was taping up a cardboard box of files for storage when I heard someone come up the hall staircase. Nobody ever came up here, not since Sam died anyway. The footsteps didn't sound like Uncle Ralph's. They were heavier and that scared me. I intended to lay low until the visitor went away but realized I'd forgotten to lock the outer door.

A large shape moved into view on the other side of the office door's opaque window. I grabbed the nearest heavy object and prepared to defend myself with the yellow pages. There was no knock before the brass knob turned and the door swung open.

"Hey, Willi. How you?" Douglas Anne Pennington said. She looked closer to fifty than sixty that day, more peachy or something. Her outfit looked like a fruit cocktail with cherry- and pineapple-colored splashes on a white silk background. It probably cost more than my house payment.

It's a wonder I didn't smell her before I saw her. Her expensive perfume, layered I'm sure with its matching high-dollar lotion and powder, was definitely in the heavyweight class. I felt my knees buckling under the punch to my sinuses.

"It's good to see you, hon," she said. "Listen, I've got a little problem. Do you mind if I sit down?"

This was a rhetorical question, seeing as how she'd

already plopped herself into the client chair. She picked at her skirt, fluffing and arranging it around her as if about to have a cotillion picture taken. I turned my head toward the apartment to take a deep breath of less-contaminated air before sitting at the desk. It was tough focusing on what she was saying, but I tried to concentrate while simultaneously conserving my oxygen supply.

"It's my ay-ex," she said.

My eyelids fluttered as they battled the fumes. "Your axe?"

She nodded. "Uh-huh. Hollis. My ay-ex husband."

"Oh. Actually, Mrs. Pennington—"

"Call me Doug," she said in a soft baritone. "Like I was saying, Hollis is giving me some trouble. I want you to help me tail him and nail him." Her eyes glistened.

"This isn't something Sam started for you, is it? I've been trying to close his unfinished cases. I don't remember seeing your name in the current file," I said, reaching down to flip through his hanging folders.

"Oh, no," she said. "This is completely new. Sam did some work for me before I divorced Hollis. Bless his heart, he was such a dear, dear boy. Not Hollis. Hollis is a skunk. I'm talking about Sam, of course." She pronounced the last word co-wuss in the manner of rich Southerners. It's a game for them, I think, to drag out words into as many syllables as possible.

I got up, walked to the apartment doorway, stuck my head in, and took another deep breath. When I turned around, Doug was picking up the little digital clock on the desk. Instead of reading the face, she looked under it, then set it down. Before I got to my chair, she repeated this procedure, while I watched, with the ashtray, the pencil holder, the mouse pad, the stapler, and the tape dispenser.

"I just like to look at things," she said in explanation as if it were the most natural thing in the world. When she went for the round file that contained clients' addresses and phone numbers, I lunged and got it first. The victory was not without cost. The file's metal feet cut two scars in the wood as I dragged it to safety.

"Doug, I don't understand. If your divorce is final, why do you want someone to follow him? I remember you told me that your ex-husband had a girlfriend, but now that he's single—"

"I don't care about that floozy. What I'm talking about is Hollis. He's gone berserk!"

"What's he done?"

"He's tearing up my house! First he broke in and went through the study. He went on a rampage, knocking over chairs, pulling down the curtains—"

"Did you call the police? Maybe it wasn't Hollis."

"Oh, it's him all right." She opened her purse and began, unnecessarily, to reapply face powder. Still looking in the compact mirror, she patted the waves of gray hair around her neck. While she primped, the office got quiet. It was hot in there. I closed my eyes and listened to the gentle whooshing of the fan in the corner, wishing it were a gulf breeze blowing over me on a quiet beach.

"But now!" Doug hollered, making me clear a good four inches above my chair. "Now he's gone too far!"

"More vandalism?"

"Huh!" she said, nodding and crossing her arms over her chest. "Well, not exactly. He's messing with my mind!"

Somehow I doubted anything so recent could account for the condition of her mind. If you mess with a mess, does it get better or worse?

"He is!" she said. "Yesterday when I got back from the beauty parlor, he had been in my den!"

Suddenly the sight of my own trashed den popped into my head. Remembering the sick feeling I had that night made me sit up and try to be more understanding. "Had he gone through the desk?"

"No."

"Thrown books and papers all over the floor?"

"No, oh no. Much worse."

"Furniture slashed?"

"No." For a moment she almost looked embarrassed. She covered it quickly with a toss of her head. The large thin hook

— 85 —

of her aristocratic nose lurched defiantly upward as she said, "Two things. He . . . well . . . first of all, he moved my *Southern Living*."

I stared.

"See, that's how I know it was him. He likes to read the outdoors articles, you know—fly-fishing, bird-hunting, deer-killing. It was the bottom one of the fan on my coffee table. Always is. He left it right on top because he knows that drives me crazy."

"You said two things."

"Yes. I did." Her voice quavered like she was about to cry. She undid the latch on her purse again. "The other," she said, "is kind of embarrassing. It's really something ladies shouldn't discuss. That's why I came to you."

I raised my eyebrows, looked at the ceiling, and said, "I'm flattered." She didn't hear me. While I was talking, she pulled out her handkerchief and gave a short loud honk.

"He's hurt me to the quick, he has!" she said. "He broke in, and . . . and . . . he came in, and he . . . he rearranged all my beautiful figurines!"

Her eyes closed tightly as she held the handkerchief to her chest and bit her bottom lip. She patted her forehead and under her nose before letting out a congested sigh.

"Now, let me see if I have this right," I said. "You're upset because Hollis—or someone—moved your knickknacks into different positions?"

Doug sprang up and back down again on the edge of her seat and said, "Yes! Yes! I knew you'd understand! They're all filthy beasts, aren't they? I'm sure you've seen more than your share, in this line of work especially. Why do we put up with men like we do? Why? Why-hy-hy?"

I shook my head.

"But they're not just knickknacks, dear." She dabbed under her eyes. "I've spent a fortune on them. Antique ballerinas, court dancers, even my sweet little bunny rabbit collection. All desecrated in those horrible . . . *positions*."

I put my hands over the bottom half of my face to keep from laughing. When I thought I was under control, I pulled the corners of my mouth down with my fingers, held them there just in case, and said, "You mean he put them in sexual positions?"

With a little gasp, she brought the handkerchief to her head and nodded. "Deviant. Perverse. Explicit positions," she said. "He's gone too far this time. It's more than a refined, genteel lady such as myself can bear! And that's why I'm gonna kill that sick sumbay-ee-yitch."

Although I told Doug over and over I wasn't a detective, she didn't listen. When I hinted that perhaps her housekeeper or even a friend with a key might be playing a joke on her, she wouldn't hear of it, insisting that Hollis was certainly the culprit.

"Look, Doug," I said. "I'm going to give you the name of a private investigator downtown. I've never met him, but Sam said he is very good. His name is Harry Dent—"

"Oh no, dear. I appreciate it, but I really was hoping you'd do it for me."

I let out a sigh and stared across the desk. I was too tired to mess around with her any longer. With much drawer slamming and desk straightening, I started gathering my things, hoping she'd take the hint. My head pounded. The session and The Bullet Incident had drained me. *Was it really a bullet?* I wasn't so sure anymore. Luanne's Fat Bird Theory was becoming easier to believe by the second.

As I stood, I realized the main cause of my headache and bad attitude wasn't Douglas Anne or the alleged bullet or the day's work. It was my fight with Jill.

Nothing I said to her at the studio was untrue. I told her just how I felt. That had probably been a bad idea in this case. I'd never meant to tell anyone, especially the girls, what I really thought—that our business had changed us for the worse.

I shouldn't have said it. I should have just said *I* had changed, without including Jill and Luanne. But the wedge was there. I suppose it had been there a long time, but I'd driven it deeper. No matter how we'd smooth it over later, from now on things would be different.

The office was quiet again. Across the desk, Douglas

Anne's poker face was too blank to read.

"Do you play cards?" I asked.

"Oh, yes. Tuesday nights are boo-ray, Friday afternoons are bridge. It's funny you should mention that. Remember the funeral where I saw you and Sam? I was wearing a purple flowered dress with a purple silk scarf and had on a—"

"I remember, I remember," I said.

"Except for one member, the same group of us has played bridge together for almost thirty years. Lucy Schaefer, the stiff's wife, played with us the first fifteen or so before she died. I still miss her."

That old joke went through my mind—"How can I miss you if you won't go away?" Slinging my purse over my shoulder, I picked up my key ring and walked to the door.

"Like sisters," Douglas Anne said. "It broke my heart to see what became of her. That dog. Not Lucy. Lucy was a dear, lovely person. I'm talking about Martin, her husband. She could have done *so* much better."

I opened the door and stood by it expectantly. Doug didn't move.

"Not that there's anything wrong with being a policeman," she said. "She married for love. Nobody could talk her out of it. We still played bridge together for many years, but otherwise she didn't socialize with the rest of us. More and more withdrawn all the time. Of course, I'm sure money was one problem . . . ."

When I flipped off the overhead light, Douglas Anne sighed and gave the desk a baleful glance. She looked down at her pocketbook then jerked her head and said, "What was that?"

"What was what?"

"I thought I saw something move in there," she said, pointing to the apartment. "Silly me. It was probably just a cat. I didn't know Sam had one."

"He doesn't," I said, stepping toward the door. Sticking my head across the threshold, I looked quickly around the living room. All was quiet.

"It was further inside. Way on in there somewhere," Douglas Anne called as I walked in. Nothing looked out of place. I peeped behind the chairs and sofa. There was no creepy feeling that someone was hiding or watching me. Still, I was ready to get out of there.

Back at the desk, Douglas Anne snapped her purse closed and stood. "It was more like a shadow really, now that I think about it. Plus these bifocals are new, so it might have been my eyes. Anyway, I must be going. It was nice seeing you."

"Wait. I'll walk down with you."

"Bye-bye," she yelled up from halfway down the stairs. She had made good time, considering her high heels. I watched her billowing dress as she stepped onto the sidewalk and turned right.

Sam's fax machine rattled. A piece of paper rolled out slowly that read, "Want to meet? Call 555-1259." It was signed "Guiness."

"Hell, naw, I don't 'want to meet'! Sober up and call like a normal person!" I yelled while kicking the desk leg. I yanked the chair out and sat heavily.

The round address file was right in front of me. Snapping my fingers, I realized Sam might have Guiness's address listed there. My hand hovered in midair while I thought, *What's wrong with this picture?* It took a while, but I finally saw it.

The card file was not where I'd last put it. Swiveling a bit, I saw the two scrape marks in the wood from my battle with Doug. Only now, the file wasn't sitting where the scratches ended anymore. I picked it up from the edge of the desk near Doug's chair. As I flipped the wheel around to G, I stopped a moment, noticing something peculiar.

"Aaaah!" I screamed. "I am such a dunce!"

Douglas Anne lied. She never saw anything move in the apartment; she just wanted me out of the room. While I was on a wild-goose chase searching for an intruder, she was busy stealing. All the cards in the S section were gone.

After taking Buddy for an extra-long walk, I was still mad at Douglas Anne Pennington. I'd brought home a worksheet from her file with her address and phone number on it. Every now and then I'd pick up the paper and look at it. By eight o'clock I couldn't stand it any longer. I dialed her number but got no answer then, or the four other times I tried. At eleven-thirty, I gave up.

Buddy's tail began thumping against his plaid doggie bed when I put the remote on the coffee table. He knows my nightly routine. At that point he races me to the bedroom, where he always wins, flopping onto the bed first.

The phone rang when I was almost asleep. It was Luanne. "Sorry to call so late," she said, "I forgot to tell you something. While you were running around the studio after our session, Jud invited us to a party tomorrow night."

Barely able to contain my excitement, I said, "I think I'll pass."

"You can't pass," she said. "It's for Jennalyn Wade. She's in town for a few days."

I cussed under my breath. "Well, maybe I have other very important plans. This is kind of short notice."

"They're just throwing it together at the last minute because Jud realized it's the twentieth anniversary of her first session. That was an important one for us, you know."

A long silence stretched between us. "In other words," I said, "I have to go."

"Yes, ma'am, you have to."

"What is tomorrow?" I asked, turning to look at my bed-side clock.

"Today," Luanne said. "I mean it's midnight now, so the party is actually tonight."

As I looked at the clock, it clicked from 11:59 to 12:00. At the same time, the date changed to July 25.

Her voice sounded low and far away with the details of the party—the time, place, and what she might wear. The date on the clock floated in and around Luanne's conversation.

I sat straight up. The date was the one on that fax from Guiness. "You were there 7-25-78" was all it had said. Up until now, I thought it had been meant for Sam. Now I could see Guiness not only knew my past, but had sent that fax to *me*.

# CHAPTER 9

MY DREAM—just before the alarm went off—was of walking down Charlotte Avenue in nothing but a slip. Macie, on her daily rounds, stopped me on the sidewalk. She said, "Here! Put this on!" then handed me a straw hat. She gave me money to buy a used dress, but I just stood there waiting for her to get it for me.

I woke up feeling stupid. While brushing my teeth, I stared at my stupid reflection. Through the stupid toothpaste foam I said, "Take charge of your life, you dingbat!" By the time I rinsed and gargled, I was determined to get those cards back from Douglas Anne whether she liked it or not. Then I'd deal with Guiness.

I saw Sam's car keys lying beside mine on the way out. Uncle Ralph wanted me to keep the muscle car, saying Sam would have wanted me to. I had no intention of doing so, but Ralph insisted I at least try it out. *Now's as good a time as any,* I thought. *If I'm going to be a take-charge badass this morning, I need to be driving wheels that demand a little respect.*

With my darkest shades on, I sat reverently in the black '68 Malibu a moment, listening to the pistons of its mighty engine. I rolled down the window and headed for the rich side of town to pay Doug a surprise visit.

On the way to Belle Meade, it occurred to me that something might have happened to Doug last night. Why else would she not answer her phone so late in the evening? She might be afraid I was on to her and let it ring in case it was me. Then again, she could be on the floor, dead from a heart attack.

Just as I was picturing Doug sprawled over an expensive

Oriental rug, she passed me on Belle Meade Boulevard, going the other way. There was no mistaking her. Her cream-colored Seville matched her blouse and jacket right down to the gold trim.

I made a U-turn at the next median opening and followed her from two cars back. *And where are we going today, Miz Doug? The mall? Bridge with the girls?* She turned left on Harding Road and then right on Davidson. I kept expecting her to go on a side street in Hillwood, a less exclusive neighborhood than Belle Meade but still out of my price range. Instead she went straight through it. At the dead end on Charlotte, I said out loud, "What are you, lost?" as she turned left toward the outskirts of town.

One car was still between us when she turned on River Road. It was a grungy-looking Gran Torino with dents all over its mostly white body. I say *mostly* because the door on the driver's side was baby blue and the front right fender had been cannibalized from a metallic brown car of the same make. The rag top was truly ragged with its black material ripped and flapping in the wind, showing rust spots underneath.

I couldn't see the guy driving. All I could tell was he had long hair and he was a real doofus, because he talked on a car phone while he drove. He finally hung up when we passed the business section at the River Road turn-off. Up ahead the road narrowed into a deep curve. I eased off the gas and fell farther back from the Torino's cockeyed bumper.

The wide body of the Cadillac took more than its share of the two-lane as the asphalt narrowed. Doug took her time—wise, considering the condition of the road. One curve after another wound between deep trenches on either side with only a few inches of gravel leeway off the shoulders. Trees and bushes crowded the far edges of the ditches and hovered over us.

Several times the car behind Doug revved its engine as if it were about to pass, even though the road had double yellow lines. The curves prevented a normal human from even thinking about passing.

Sadly, the Torino's driver was abnormally subhuman. His muffler roared as he rode the Seville's bumper, then jerked toward the left lane. Twice he swerved back split seconds before an oncoming car whooshed by us. On his third attempt he didn't jerk behind her again, but thundered around Doug. Her brake lights flashed as she slowed to let him by.

*Good riddance*, I thought. His back tires squealed around her. But instead of speeding up to pass, he drifted slightly to the left, still driving alongside, then yanked his wheel hard right.

His front end smashed the side of Doug's headlight. Her right wheel thudded off the two-inch shoulder, but to her credit, she recovered quickly, pushing her tank of a car right back at him.

Up ahead in a stretch of straight road, I saw the entrance to a rock quarry. What looked like a twenty-ton dump truck full of gravel had cleared the gate and turned onto the road. It was heading toward us.

I couldn't believe what I was seeing. Even with a head-on collision only moments away, the Torino tried to run Doug into the ditch again. He floored it and smacked her again, this time with almost the full length of his car. Off the shoulder, she skidded with her tire half in gravel and half hanging off the ridge of the ditch. The dump truck's air brakes whistled their highest pitch as it tried to stop, while the Torino's driver punched his accelerator, escaping with one last screech of steel against the Seville. Zooming around the next curve, the lunatic with the crooked bumper disappeared.

After side-slamming the Torino in defense, Doug cut her steering wheel to avoid sliding into the dump truck. Never slowing, she drove ahead about twenty yards, made a sharp turn by the next mailbox, and climbed a steep driveway.

I followed her up the long bumpy drive and around the back of a ranch-style house on top of the hill. On the porch, an old man sat in a rocker with a shotgun leaning against the house behind him. A collection of brown earthenware jugs sat next to what looked like a still. On top of the metal contraption, a dark brew bubbled through a glass coil.

As I took in the scene, I was glad I was there with Doug. She didn't need to be up here alone. I figured she only came here to get somewhere safe and call the police.

The man stood with the help of a cane and hobbled down the porch steps toward us. Maybe he wasn't quite so old as I'd thought, but he still looked mean and half-crazy to me. Doug got out of the Cadillac and brushed off her suit while inspecting the damage.

I was about to ask if she was all right when the old man said, "You Mrs. Pennington?" My mouth froze in an open hanging position as she acknowledged him and fluffed her hair. He said, "Who is that?" pointing the tip of his cane to me.

Doug turned and jumped when she saw me. "What are you doing here?" she demanded.

"Are you all right? I saw that guy try to run you off the road."

"You saw that? He nearly killed me! Ignorant rednecks . . . oh . . . excuse me," she said to the man. "No offense."

"None taken," he said, smiling. A gleam of intelligence sparkled in his eyes. "This happened on the way here?" He felt the scrapes and dents in the door and whistled. "That's gonna cost you. Why, the paint job alone—"

"Look, excuse me for interrupting," I said. "Doug, I thought you might need my help. Obviously you don't, so I'll be on my way as soon as you hand over the cards."

At first she looked puzzled then caught my drift. "I don't know what you're talking about," she lied.

"Cut the crap," I said in as menacing a tone as I could muster. "Just give them back."

The old man straightened up and noticed Sam's car for the first time. He gave me a look I couldn't decipher, then busted out laughing.

I stared into Doug's designer bifocals. She huffed, opened her purse, and said, "Oh, all right. Here. I don't need them anymore anyway."

"Apology accepted," I said and marched back to Sam's

car. As I put it in reverse, the old man hollered and waved his cane at me. I couldn't hear what he said and didn't care. *They're both lunatics*, I thought. Whatever they were up to, they could have at it.

On my way home, the sight of Doug and the old crippled guy became more and more perplexing. What business could Doug have with him? Was he the reason she'd lifted those cards? Past the intersection of White Bridge Road and Harding, I took a left. Sam's car needed a fill-up, so I stopped at the Mapco where I'd seen Julie and Stephanie Schaefer on my great stakeout attempt.

*What the hell*, I thought. *I have nothing better to do.* After filling the tank, I turned right onto Kenner, then into the last office building's parking lot.

It was the same place I'd parked when Sam had me watch her house. My eyes kept going up to the rearview mirror every few seconds. It was a crazy, impossible wish but I kept doing it—hoping I'd see Sam there smiling and waving, the way he had only a few hours before his death.

The front door of the Schaefers' house opened. Automatically I reached for the glove compartment and found Sam's binoculars. It was Stephanie. I could see her clearly right down to the freckles on her nose. Her long blonde hair was squashed on top by a floppy denim hat. She wore a tie-dyed blouse over a crinkled skirt that revealed only bare ankles and clunky sandals. *Peace, man. Like, hand me another brownie.*

She grinned from ear to ear. Her arms swung with each bouncy-bouncy step. Oh yeah, she was high. But at nine-thirty in the morning? Maybe she had a perfectly legal mind-bending herbal supplement with her breakfast.

Making an exaggerated snap of her fingers, she twirled around as if she'd just remembered something. By the time she reached the door, she looked like she'd forgotten what she'd forgotten. With a shrug she resumed her happy little walk and stopped for a moment to chat with the gladiola.

I scooted down in the seat and stuck my elbow out the

open window to let my left arm rest. I nearly jumped out of my skin when I jabbed into something fleshy. My scream made the man who had sneaked up on me jump, too. His stomach tightened as he skipped back a half-step from the car. He was about my age, a little pudgy, and wore a business suit.

When we recovered, we both started laughing. "Looking for something?" he said, indicating the binoculars.

"No! No, no, I'm just . . . seeing if they work," I said, fumbling around trying to wrap the cord around its center and put them away. The glove compartment door wouldn't open until I gave it a good belt.

"That's funny," he said, still laughing, "because it looked to me like you were spying on my sister's house." He beamed good-naturedly while stretching the words out in a skeptical drawl.

With an inner groan, I recognized Martin Schaefer Jr. "Your sister lives on this street? Wow, no kidding! It sure is a nice sister . . . uh, street . . . is real nice . . . your sister's street here."

"I know you!" he said. "Billie, right?"

"Pretty close," I said. "*Willi*, actually. With a *W*." As in *What the hell am I doing here?*

He nodded and said, "Right. Yeah, I stop by and check on Stephanie sometimes before I go to the office. She's there by herself now, you know. Julie and I worry about her. So when I drove by and saw binoculars trained on the house, I figured I better stop and check it out." His voice shook with laughter as it raised to a practiced climax of incredulity. *Ho boy*, I thought. *Of all things, I've been caught red-handed by a damn lawyer. He is* not *going to let me go.*

It's times like this I think of Bear. From out of nowhere, his image came to me—Bear Bryant in his checked hat and a sport coat, striding along the sideline—seeing him the way a football player might from the huddle.

I had no idea how I was going to wiggle out of this one. All I can say is Martin Jr.'s southern disarmament tactics gave me a strange charge way down deep, like a distant horn calling me to battle.

Martin Jr. was good. He was smart, well-educated, and made his living by out-talking people. His fake farm-boy shuck-and-jive had probably dismantled many a weaker soul.

But as I watched his smug grin become more confident, I thought, *That bull ain't gonna work with me. For once, you've chosen the wrong weapon, counselor. I may not be smarter, but I'm a whole lot southerner than you.*

His boyish face peered into the car. Cocking my head to the side, I returned his look of naïveté. In my mind, the crowd cheered as the offense trotted onto the field.

"Hang on just one taaah-ny little second," I drawled. I rolled up the window, grabbed my purse, and opened the door. I couldn't resist making him wait while I put on lipstick in the rearview mirror. After much lip blotting and teeth checking, I shouldered my bag and slid off the seat. *Thirteen . . . twenty-five . . . hut . . . hut.*

With a cheerful pop, I locked the door with the flat of my hand. I stood as close as possible to him and gave him a four-star grit-eatin' grin, then said, "Stephanie seemed so ni-i-ice. It's sweet of you to look after her. Lord knows there aren't many men in this world who take time for that kind of a thing any-*mo*-wer."

Martin Jr. opened his mouth to speak, but I touched his arm and kept talking. "Julie's so lucky to have you—a fine, thoughtful, handsome man that loves his family. *And* makes a good living, that's important too, let's not forget that!" *Looking long . . . looking long . . . where's my man . . . ?*

He looked at the ground again, shaking his head, and said, "Ah, I don't know about all that." When he looked up and took another breath, I grabbed hold of his arm just above the elbow à la Doug, pinched the fire out of it, and said, "But now, listen. I have to run." I looked at my watch, made a big show of adjusting a difficult bra strap, then stepped toward the office building. With a half turn back, I said, "Oh, and hey, I'm sorry I worried you with those silly old binoculars." I covered my mouth with both hands and giggled. "See, this isn't my car. I borrowed it and was looking around in it, being nosy." Another step, another two away from him. "When I saw those in the glove box—I don't know, I just tried them out I guess, right when you happened to drive by."

He was nodding now and giggling along with me. His finger wiped the corner of his eye. "I understand," he said, chuckling. "No problem. Ha-ha, you really got me!" He touched the corners of his other eye. "Oh-ho, me me me. Who's your appointment with?"

*Block! I need a blocker!* My heart stopped but I never quit smiling. One name came to mind as I pictured a legendary Tide guard holding the line for me. "Hannah," I said confidently. "John Hannah. At Soundgate Audio Consultants. You know John?" Behind Martin Jr., a large brick sign supplied the name of a legitimate business inside the building.

His eyebrows furrowed as he stuck his hands in his pockets. "No, I don't believe I do."

*She's at the twenty, the fifteen . . . .* I held up my hand in good-bye and walked backwards toward the building. "Tell Julie to give me a call sometime, you hear? Take care now, hon. Bye-bye." *Dear God, please don't let the front door be locked.* It was early still. Only two cars other than ours were parked in the front lot. Doing my best not to look back, I gripped the rails going up the steps.

Why did I have to give him a company name anyway? I began picturing Martin Jr. calling Soundgate to check out my story. The odds were in the bazillions for them to have a John Hannah working there.

When the knob turned, The Million-Dollar Band kicked fast and furious into the Tide fight song. Clicking the door shut behind me, my arms flew straight up. *Touchdown, Al-a-ba-ma!* I buzzed the song's melody through my lips like a kazoo while marching and playing air trombone. The crowd roared and stomped the bleachers in time. The stands were a frenzied blur of crimson and white.

A prune-faced secretary stuck her head out a doorway. She looked at me suspiciously and said, "May I help you?"

"Oh. Excuse me. I'm looking for the Soundgate offices?"

Her look told me she suspected as much. Without blinking, she pointed slowly down the hall and watched as I walked by. No kazoo. No trombone.

The Soundgate office was locked. *Thank you, Lord*, I thought, returning to the front door. I peeped out the lobby's curtain to make sure Martin Jr. was gone, and drove home to lay low until time for Jennalyn's party.

Three stretch limos lined the studio drive at Jud Sherrill's complex on the river. This tells you how late I was. If the limos are already there, the party is about over. Stars want to make grand entrances and will do so only when everybody else is there to see them. Jennalyn was no exception.

I almost didn't go. After having such a weird morning with Douglas Anne, her hillbilly friend, and Martin Schaefer, I walked Buddy and then crashed for most of the day. I dragged around the house, putting off getting ready for as long as possible.

But Luanne was right; we owed Jennalyn. It would be disrespectful for me not to go. I'd stay thirty, forty-five minutes tops, say hello to her, a few others, and duck out.

For such a spur-of-the-moment event, there was a huge turnout. Jen's career swing toward Hollywood had really brought out the sleaze. I walked by row after row of BMWs, Jags, and Range Rovers, having to leave the Malibu out in the lower forty.

The waiting lounge and adjoining veranda were packed. I sidestepped that area. Down the photo gallery hall leading to the studios, I could see Jill holding court from the middle of a group of men. I spoke to a few people here and there until I reached them, standing around the picture of us at Jen's first session.

"It's about time you got here," Jill said, folding her arms across her chest. Excuses went through my head as she looked at me expectantly. I couldn't think of a snappy comeback.

"Look," I said, "I'm here. Where's Jennalyn?"

Jill jerked her head toward a room just beyond us, which

seemed to be the heart of the party. People started pushing out of it, including Luanne, who joined us. When the crowd divided down the middle, we soon saw the responsible Moses. A big black guy in a perfectly tailored gray suit scanned faces while clearing a path for Jennalyn.

Coming toward us, she was like a model walking the runway. Her clothes, hair, and makeup were perfect. The dress, a floor-length shift, had a plunging neckline and was made from a midnight blue brocade. It was a beautiful color that complemented her lighter blue eyes. They sparkled in camera flashes as she posed for a moment, then walked to us.

There were no awkward moments. Jennalyn hugged us all, then stood between me and Jill with her elbows looped through ours. She had never been haughty with us, not even after the movies and the cosmetics deal. She looked lovingly at the giant photo of us together at her first session.

"That picture kept me going through some pretty rough times," Jennalyn said, her soft Indiana accent barely noticeable. "I kept a small one just like it on my dresser for years."

Someone called to Jen from across the room. She looked up and waved to Blaine Sherrill and Rick Crawford. Her hand went to her throat to touch her necklace as she looked at the old photo again. In it, she wore the same little chain with blue beads on either side of a larger engraved one hanging in the center.

"This is my lucky charm. Those two found it," she said, indicating Blaine and Rick, "working backstage at the Ryman. They were about to throw it away, but I said, 'Wait! That might have been Patsy Cline's!' I knew it wasn't, of course. But I felt like it was meant for me, like it would bring me good luck."

Blaine, now standing next to his father, motioned for Jennalyn to join them. "Excuse me, folks," she said. With his arm extended, the bodyguard made a path for Jen again through the crowd.

After kissing Jud, Rick, and Blaine, she faced us and smiled from across the room. We all watched as she touched the chain lightly again. I could read her lips as she said, "I was telling them about my present."

Blaine Sherrill worked in his father's studio, then took over his dad's music publishing company after college. Lately, he had branched into production, earning a couple of gold records on his own. I remembered what a crush Blaine had on Jen back then. Now, they made a beautiful couple. As I watched them hug, I had to admit I was envious. It made me miss Sam.

A few minutes later, Jill reached out to turn me and Luanne toward Jennalyn. She was motioning for the three of us to join her at the hall to the studios.

"Pit stop," Jen said. Pat, her assistant, walked briskly ahead of us and unlocked a door. It opened on a hall with an elevator, a private one to Jud's penthouse office.

After going up three floors, the elevator opened into a huge outdoorsy room. It was like a lodge complete with fireplace and deer heads. To our far left, floor-to-ceiling shelves and cabinets were behind a giant desk, the only indication this was an office. On either side of the hearth across from us, the wall was glass with French doors opening onto a wide upper porch.

Jennalyn grabbed her purse off a couch and started rummaging through it. "While you're all together, I wanted to ask if you would be able to do a show with me," she said. "I'm doing a 'live' taped show for cable in a couple of months. I'd fly you out to L.A. for about a week. We'll rehearse four days with the band, then tape for two—possibly three—days. If you're all interested."

I could hear the excitement in Jill's voice as she said, "I've got my book right here, let me check it." Luanne perked up too. This would be very big bucks for us, plus the TV exposure always brought us more work here at home. Jill went into her business mode, taking down specifics in her date book as Pat read them off.

Jen and Luanne walked to the bathroom, talking and laughing together. As Jill and Pat discussed money, I turned away from them and stepped to the glass wall.

Suddenly I froze. All the chatter in the room sounded like

it had been sucked into a tunnel. I realized I was moving slowly along the glass, much slower than normal. When I got to the latch, I turned it and walked through the French doors onto the porch in a daze.

Below us, a few scattered lights along the paths lit up the rose garden. From Jud's railing, the bench at the garden's center would be a clear and easy shot.

Hands gripped my shoulders close to my neck. I drew in a sharp breath, thinking I was about to be throttled, or thrown over the ledge, but it was just Jill. She stood behind me and followed my gaze. In a coarse whisper, she over-enunciated each word she said through clenched jaws. "*Do not say anything. Do you understand? Do *not* mess this up. Whatever you think happened, do *not* talk about it in front of Jennalyn. Do you hear me?*"

There was more in her tone than urgency. Although I knew she was right, that becoming hysterical would serve no purpose, she made me want to scream even more. Chills were already running up my spine before Jill spoke. Now I shivered not only because she still doubted me, but because she could not keep the hate out of her voice.

I nodded. She loosened her grip, then pushed me ahead of her into the office. When the doors shut behind her, I blocked her way for a moment. I wanted her to look me in the face while we stood right there, next to a mahogany gun cabinet full of rifles.

I was polite but said little on the ride downstairs. Before the elevator completely opened, I squeezed through, hoping to make a quick getaway. I had taken one step into the hall before ramming right into Jud Sherrill, waiting to go up.

"Whoa, hoss! What's your hurry?" he said. Any other time, I wouldn't have minded his hands grabbing my arms or patting and rubbing my back, or being held close against him in a bear hug. I trusted him. I *used* to trust him.

"Move it, Willi," Jill said from the back of the elevator. "Move it *now*."

She didn't have to worry. Even if I wanted to say something to Jud, I couldn't. My breath was coming in short gasps. My mind was completely blank as I stared up at him. His bristly beard stuck out a bit defiantly, I thought, but his manner was jovial and carefree.

In the corner of my eye, I saw the bodyguard holding the elevator door open. "Excuse me," he said as he and Jennalyn walked behind us. Jud released me, almost like a shove, to turn his attention to Jen and the girls. After a few pleasantries, Jud got in the elevator and pushed a button. I lingered behind the others and said to him, "That office is fabulous."

He held up his hand. "Thanks, hon."

I couldn't help myself. As the panel moved to close, I said, "And that's a helluva gun collection. Done any deer shooting lately?"

He smiled. "No," he said. "Dear."

And the door snapped shut.

I walked straight to the bar. With my drink and an extra napkin, I walked into the crowd. My plan was to speak to a few people then make a quick exit.

Thirty minutes later, I was still trying to leave. I kept running into friends I hadn't seen in a long time. Some were writers, others were singers I worked with on occasion. In fact, I think everyone I'd ever worked with wanted to stop and talk a while.

My head started hurting about the time I reached the end of the photo gallery hallway. After shooting the breeze with some guy who apparently knew me well but whose name I couldn't recall, I threw back the last sip of my drink. We stood in front of the first picture of Jud at age fourteen. It was the one where his baby face is upturned toward a huge old RCA microphone.

I thought I saw his lips move. I'm talking about Jud's, in the picture. While I watched they did it again, like he was singing. I blinked hard and shook my head. The old microphone swayed back and forth. Jud swayed along with it.

I couldn't remember if I had eaten supper. By the time I reached the front door, I couldn't remember anyone I'd just talked to.

I almost tripped trying to walk down the outside steps, and probably would have if one of a group of smokers hadn't caught me. Once on level ground, I managed to walk a little better through the parking lot.

Someone helped me find Sam's car. I let whoever it was have my keys since I couldn't connect with the lock. When I sat down I could hardly hold my eyes open. My stomach felt queasy as the scent of a strong cologne filled the car's interior.

I couldn't figure out where the steering wheel was until I heard the engine start and realized I wasn't in the driver's seat. My head wouldn't turn to see who was. Just before blacking out, it finally hit me—*I've been drugged.*

# CHAPTER 10

*A FULL ORCHESTRA accompanied my acrobatics as I flew high in the air wearing a red cape and tights. I began a routine of somersaults to the 1812 Overture, complete with real cannon fire. Acknowledging the crowd far below with a Queen Elizabeth wave, I opened wide for a toothy smile. I tasted salt. Instead of air, water rushed over my tongue and I realized I wasn't flying at all, but swimming upward from the ocean floor.*

*The symphony played on with the cannons' parts becoming depth charges that sunk past me, then exploded in tempo. Spinning in easy pirouettes as I ascended, I tilted my head all the way back and gargled the melody.*

*I could see a puddle of light overhead. I swam up, surfacing in the percussion section as mallets pounded kettledrums. All the cymbals fell off their stands, crashed across the drums' skins in a horrendous clatter, then sank. With my head bobbing, I shook the water out of my eyes and looked across the horizon. The orchestra floated in black water and drifted farther and farther away . . . .*

My eyelids felt heavy as they fluttered between dark dream and dark sky. A fine mist of rain covered my face. I was flat on my back, feeling a hard, itchy bumpiness underneath me. The spray changed to occasional droplets that splattered all over me. One hit my cheekbone, sending a featherlight scurry of legs up across my eye and forehead.

A sudden crash of thunder jolted me fully awake. I sat up with a start, unable to see anything in the pitch dark. Something slimy crawled across the back of my hand. I shook it off and began brushing away leaves or bugs that tickled my face and hair.

In a brief flash of lightning, I could see I was sitting on grass. Beside me, my hand rested on a clump of dirt. Left in darkness again, I clambered to my knees with difficulty. My side was killing me, making me double over in pain. I fell forward onto my hands to rest a while before attempting to stand.

The rain fell harder now. My hair was flattened and dripping. I combed it straight back with my fingers and wiped the water off my face. My jaw hurt. It was tender and swollen as if someone had belted me. Running my tongue over my teeth, I tasted blood.

As I strained to make out the low shapes around me, lightning ripped across the sky in a long series of jags. For a moment I couldn't hear or see. The thunder was bone-jarring and the white flashes temporarily blinded me.

As my eyes adjusted and the sky continued to arc with electricity, my surroundings became familiar. Horror stiffened my body. I knew exactly where I was. About three feet away stood a granite tombstone with the name *Robbins* etched in it. Someone had stretched me out beside Sam's grave.

Overhead, a deep-pitched explosion of colliding thunderclouds muted my scream. A message had been left for me. In the swift on-and-off strobe-like lightning, it flashed like neon atop the mound of wet dirt. Dead flowers circled a sheet of white paper where rain pelted the words *DROP IT, BITCH, OR YOU'RE NEXT.*

My chest and shoulders shook violently as I stumbled backwards. The heels of my pumps sunk into the soft earth and I fell flat, the ground pressing water through my dress. My ribs hurt so badly I couldn't push straight up. I rolled over on my stomach. Letting my face fall into the wet blades of grass, I wanted to stay there, to hide, not believe the unbelievable—*Someone has beaten me.* I embraced the ground, wishing I could be swallowed by it as curtains of blowing rain shirred over me.

With another great boom, the bottom fell out of the clouds. If not for the prodding of the storm, I might still be lying there not caring where I was or if I caught pneumonia. Struggling to my feet, I spit rain and tried to wipe my face dry. I remembered seeing a police station nearby the day of Sam's funeral. I'd have to get there.

I held my shoes tightly across my chest. With a slow turn I looked all around me. Evenly spaced across little hills and valleys, thousands of grave markers stretched in all directions. It would be a long walk to the main road.

I had no choice but to go slowly. It didn't really matter since I was already soaked. My ankle hurt with each step but I didn't dare stop to rest. I was afraid I wouldn't be able to make myself get back up. And it would be hours, maybe half a day, before anyone might come this way and find me.

Rounding the last curve, I saw the entrance's brick wall ahead. Rain sparkled around the globes of tall street lamps, casting an eerie orange glow over the cemetery. I gasped. Parked in the wall's shadow was the Malibu.

The keys hung in the ignition. With a quick glance, I checked the backseat. No one there. As soon as I slid in, I locked the door behind me. With the heater on full blast, I sat gripping the wheel until my arms quit shaking. My purse sat in the passenger's seat.

The streets were deserted. I kept going when I passed the Berry Hill police station. All I wanted was to get home and get in bed. It was 3:52 A.M. when I passed the bank down the block from my condo. When I turned the deadbolt on my front door, my VCR read 3:56.

After quickly stripping off wet clothes, I wrapped up in my tattered pink terry cloth robe. I took a couple of extra-strength aspirins, rinsed out my mouth, and toweled my hair dry. At 4:04 A.M., I eased onto the end of the bed. Buddy licked my cheeks, let out a big sigh, and flopped his leg across my arm. I was out by 4:05.

Detective Bracken sat patiently in his office, smoking as he waited for my story. I had called him when I woke up, about one in the afternoon, half-hoping he wouldn't be in.

His big frame seemed as wide as his desk. The neck of

his shirt was open, with his tie hanging on the coatrack next to his shoulder holster. Dark rings emphasized the puffiness of his eyes, giving him the look of one who never gets enough sleep.

As I talked, he sat still, taking in every word. Only the smoke moved, first curling around his rough fingers then trailing upward like incense from the palm of a contemplative Buddha. It spread wider in front of his face with his graying blond hair outlining the little screen of smoke.

I remembered the night Sam was killed, how Bracken instilled fear in those who worked for him, then was so gentle with me. He was doing it again. There was a kind of tenderness in his actions—how he waited for me in the lobby of the station, how he ushered me up. His eye contact with others was chilling, but to me he spoke softly. That and his complete attention jarred me. Although I considered the possibility it could be an act, one formulated to extract the most information from women, my instincts told me differently. Maybe I was kidding myself, but at least he listened and seemed to take me seriously.

After the part about waking up in the cemetery, he ran his finger down a list of phone numbers taped on his desk. He spoke with someone at the Berry Hill station, asking if they'd had any unusual activity last night. After hanging up, he said, "You didn't notice anything in the car?"

I shook my head. "I looked before coming here."

"No ideas who might've driven you there? Nothing suspicious at the party?"

I closed my eyes and took a deep breath. "There is something else," I said. I got up and started pacing behind my chair. I looked at the pictures on his wall, read the spines of books on a small shelf. I found myself hesitating to mention Jud Sherrill or anyone specifically. What if I was wrong?

"I think I was shot at," I said and told him about the rose garden, Jud's balcony, and his gun cabinet. "But things have been so crazy, so confusing. I'm not even sure it really happened. My friends certainly don't think so. I didn't find a bullet hole in the tree, or even a bullet anywhere around it."

Bracken shrugged. "Most likely you wouldn't. They can travel a lot farther than most people think. It probably went in the river."

"I don't know. I guess it all sounds pretty far-fetched to you," I said.

"Oh, I believe you," he said. "That swollen jaw tells me something is going on."

I felt like an idiot. It was sore but wasn't swollen that much. I thought I had covered it well enough with extra makeup to keep it from showing.

"This party," he said, "tell me about it." He stuck his cigarette in his mouth and took a pen out of his shirt pocket.

"It was just a party," I said, thinking I had nothing to say. I ended up telling him almost every detail of the room, the people I saw, and what they wore. The more I talked, the better I felt. Bracken should have been a psychiatrist.

When I started talking about Jennalyn and her first session, I noticed Bracken's hand moved slower across the page. I paused a moment when his pen stopped, tapped the paper a few times, then drew a big arrow. He looked off in the distance and started smiling.

"What is it?" I asked.

"I remember that. Geez, has it been twenty years?" He laughed and resumed writing.

"How do you remember? Did you work in the music business then?"

He laughed again and said, "No. I was on limited duty working the booking desk. Right before the end of my shift one night, there was a hubbub over a small-time drug bust at Jud's old studio off Music Row."

He shook his head and looked out the window. "It's too small of a connection to Sam. Nothing came of it. Nothing good anyway." With a broad stroke, he crossed off a line on his paper.

"I don't get it," I admitted. "What connection? What's Sam got to do with it?"

His brow wrinkled as he drew in a long drag. "He was still on the force then. It was Sam's bust."

Bracken read the bewilderment on my face. "He didn't tell you he was a cop?" he asked.

Stunned, I shook my head. Why hadn't he told me? All the signs had been there—attending a retired policeman's funeral, the way he joked and looked at ease with the other cops there. "He didn't talk about his past, only that he had traveled around before settling here again."

"Did he tell you his big sister died of an overdose? She ran away from home at seventeen. Two years later, she was found dead in an L.A. flophouse. Sam was just a kid. His parents were killed in a car accident not long afterwards. That's when he moved to Nashville to live with Ralph and Lucille."

"You've known them a long time," I said, remembering how Ralph had spoken to him.

"Yeah. I grew up in the same neighborhood. Ralph knew my folks and older brothers. I went straight to the police academy after school. Sam joined the Navy first."

"I knew about that."

Bracken nodded. "He was a great guy and a damn good cop. That bust was clean. He had them dead to rights, and the thing was, the kid from California—"

"Rick Crawford?"

"Was that his name? Yeah, Crawford." He scribbled again. "He would have led to bigger suppliers. It should have put Sam over the top with a promotion. The way it ended up, Crawford got off scot-free. Sam never got over it. He was so disgusted he turned in his badge."

"If Rick was caught red-handed, how did he get out of it?"

"One of the other boys was Jud Sherrill's son. While they were being brought to the station, Jud was on his way to the mayor's house. Mayor Foley was having his weekly poker game. Jud hauled him and Judge Will Clements downtown to the lock-up. It was late. The mayor and Judge Will were both drunk. They got the chief of police out of bed and everybody stood around yelling and cussing at each other.

"They struck a deal. With the strings Jud pulled, all three were eventually released. When Sam heard what was going on, he lost it. He stormed into the chief's office and called him every name in the book. He was put on suspension, then finally quit."

Bracken and I sat without talking while everything sank in. His phone rang, and after a brief conversation he hung up and turned back to me.

"You look tired," he said. "Ms. Taft, my advice is to take a vacation. Get out of town for a few days. Forget about wrapping up Sam's cases. By the time you get back, maybe whatever you've stirred up will have settled back down."

"But I'm not working on anything!" I said. "All I've done is bill a few people and pack files. I swear, I have no idea what's going on."

He stood and said, "Let me walk you out. I'd like to have a look in the car, if you don't mind. It's a miracle whoever left you out there didn't steal that Malibu. I would have."

We walked across the street to the parking garage. After a quick look under the seats and around the outside, Bracken held the door open then shut me inside.

"Go home and get some rest. I think I'll take a ride over to Berry Hill," he said. He took a card out of his wallet and wrote another number on the back. "This is my pager number. If you need me, call. Day or night." I took it and thanked him.

"What I'd like you to do," he said, "is go through Sam's paper records one more time for me. Write down the names of any clients that work in the music business in any capacity. Anyone at all you recognize. We still have his backup disks here. I'll start looking through those again. Let me know what you find. Before you go on vacation."

I thought about the beach while I drove. Bracken was right. I'd make reservations when I got home. But first, I had one more stop to make.

Heading west on Charlotte from the Criminal Justice Center, I turned left toward Ben West Library, the main branch downtown. A homeless man preceded me into the lobby of the circa 1950 building, styled in what I would call Old Modern. I stopped at the information desk, then made my way to the stacks.

The basement was crammed with shelves, mostly metal with a few rows of scratched and dinged wooden ones. Cardboard file boxes of all sizes were piled one on top of the other around the walls. While the librarian, a lady with short cropped hair and dangly earrings, looked for what I'd requested, I tried to decipher the hieroglyphics printed on a few nearby labels. In less than a minute, she closed a file drawer and handed me an envelope. Turning on a tabletop projector, she left me alone in a musty corner, her African-print skirt swooshing as she climbed the stairs.

Weeks flew by my eyes as the microfiche moved. Pulling up the date of the drug bust in the old newspaper files was no problem. Unfortunately, I found just what I expected—nothing. Although I knew the charges against the boys had been dropped, I had hoped for some mention of the bust.

During that time, all the reporters' attentions focused on two more sensational stories. One was the rape and murder of a local fifteen-year-old girl, whose photograph nearly broke my heart. Just as prominent in the news was a particularly nasty mudslinging campaign for the governor's office. The pictures of Mayor Foley, leading in the race at the time, showed him as drunk as the one in Jud's studio did. He was dressed well but his eyes and veined nose said he'd been to a few too many fund-raiser cocktail parties.

I scanned three or four days further ahead to see if maybe Jennalyn's first session picture had been printed. No luck there either. Of course, she was an unknown at the time. I guess she didn't rate as newsworthy, even if Mayor Foley was in the picture, too.

A sudden thump, like a shoe hitting against a bookcase, jerked my attention away from the screen. I turned and froze in my chair, listening. The room was quiet except for the humming of the microfiche screen. Rather than the absence of sound, it felt like someone *being* quiet. My back and shoulders tensed. With one motion, I grabbed my purse and stood, easing around the chair.

My heart raced. I couldn't see anything but boxes and

old thick books in any direction. Hiding from someone would be easy in here. The shelves loomed larger than before, closing in on me. *Get a grip. You're just paranoid.* In my mind, Jill's voice was loud and clear as I pictured her folding her arms and giving me a cross look.

I reached down to click off the projector. As I gathered the film and quickly stuffed the envelope, I thought I heard a soft scraping noise. I froze again. All was still except for the envelope, which shook in my hand. From the corner I scanned the nearest shelves, thinking it wouldn't take much of a shove to send them crashing down. Imagining the weight made my neck duck involuntarily. I raced up the stairs, slinging the microfiche on the information desk as I ran outside.

My one attempt to laugh off the hasty retreat from the library turned into a crying fit on the way home. By the time I pulled into my driveway, I'd decided I needed to take a nap for a few weeks.

Buddy had other ideas. He greeted me at the door with his leash in his mouth and a smile in his eyes. *My therapist.* I snapped the lead on his collar and let him drag me around the neighborhood until almost dusk. Afterward I stood in the shower a good thirty minutes until the fog in the bathroom was so dense it stung my eyes.

Luanne called just as I was polishing off a chicken burrito TV dinner. "What are you wearing tomorrow?"

"For what?" I said as I set the tray down for Buddy to lick. He loves Mexican.

"I knew you'd forget," she said. "I'm worried about you, Willi, I really am. You used to not be like this. Lately you've been so touchy, and acting weird, and forgetful . . . ."

While Einstein enumerated my faults, I reached for my date book. Flipping quickly to the following day's schedule, I tapped my finger on my only session that day. Jill and Luanne were booked on it too.

"I ain't forgot nothin'," I said in a backwoods accent. "And I have not given the smallest fraction of a thought as to what

I'll wear to . . . David Payton's damn session tomorrow at two o'clock."

"And you've been cussing an awful lot," she said. "You cuss when you get touchy."

"Luanne," I said. I took a deep breath, realizing I shouldn't be taking out my frustrations, or "touchiness," or whatever, on her. "Was there a real reason you called?"

"I just wanted to remind you, that's all," she said. "And see what you were going to wear. And make sure it wasn't too sexy because I want David to ask *me* out, not you."

Luanne had been working on David Payton since he first moved here from Los Angeles. He had quite a bit of clout in town, was a super-nice guy, and most importantly, he was single.

"I promise," I said. "I'll wear a church dress, how's that?"

"You don't have to go that far. As long as it's something nice. And as long as you . . . ." She hesitated. "And be there on time."

"As long as I what?"

"As long as you be nice. I just want you to be in a good mood, that's all."

While I pondered that, Buddy nudged the TV dinner tray across the floor. I held it still for him and said, "I'll do my very best, old friend."

After a short silence on the line, she said, "Jill said maybe we could all go eat supper when we're through."

"Sure. Whatever y'all want to do. Listen, I'm tired. I think I'll go on to bed. You know, rest up so I'll be in a real good mood tomorrow. See you at two."

When we hung up, I went straight to the kitchen. I stuck one chocolate chip cookie in my mouth, put the bag under my arm, and poured myself a glass of milk. Enough screwing around. It was time to get down to serious business.

I took the plastic grocery bag containing Sam's stash of cassettes from under the sink. Slipping my wrist through the holes, I picked up my milk and went back to the living room. When I dumped the contents in the middle of the floor, Buddy got excited. He started pawing the cassettes, thinking we were about to play a game. Buddy likes board games, especially checkers since he can slide them easily with his nose. He wins more often than I like to admit.

When I pushed PLAY to listen to the first cassette, the voice took me by surprise. Buddy barked and wagged his tail, then lay down close to the stereo's speaker.

Sam spoke over the speakers as if he were in the room with us interviewing a client. *Interview* is a loose term. From the sound quality and offhand way he extracted information, I'd say he had neglected to ask permission to record this conversation. He probably had put his mini-recorder in his jacket pocket.

I sat in the floor for hours with Buddy flopped over on me. One thing was different about these cases—none of them appeared to be about divorce, the usual motive people had for hiring Sam. With a pen and pad ready, I kept expecting to hear clues that would jump out at me and make sense of Sam's murder.

But after listening to tape after tape, nothing struck me as pertinent. There wasn't one mention of anyone I knew, in or out of the music business.

# CHAPTER 11

BEFORE GOING TO DAVID PAYTON'S SESSION the next afternoon, I stopped by Sam's office.

The red light of the message machine blinked on the desktop. While I listened to a man who wanted his wife followed, I looked over at the fax machine, a plain gray box Sam proudly told me he made himself. A single page lay at its mouth with very little writing on it.

The second phone message, a female version of the first, played while I read. Before the suspicious wife could say "cheating," I hit my hand down hard on top of the answering machine several times until it finally shut off. I needed to concentrate on the words in front of me.

The fax read, "I was right under your nose. You were too out of it to see me. Don't worry, we'll meet again. Next time, I keep the car." It was signed "Guiness."

As before, only the time and date sent were printed at the top. No name or return phone number. How could he rig that? This guy did not want to be traced. I had no idea who he really was or how to find out.

The only certainty was the tight clutch of fear returning to the pit of my stomach. *Guiness was the one who drugged me.*

From the front doors of Music Max, I heard distant cackling like a party going on deep inside the studio. I wasn't surprised to find Jill and Luanne the centers of attention as they yukked it up with the producer, David Payton.

The room got quiet when I walked in. The engineer, an ugly little guy with glasses and no chin, turned to me from the tape machine and said, "It's about time you got here."

Our session was set for 2:00 P.M. I looked at my watch. It was 1:45.

Jill and Luanne laughed, knowing my history with Tim "Possum" Davenport and knowing I'd be in no mood for such bull. I smiled broadly, determined to play nice.

"How are you, David?" I said, greeting the producer first. His Hawaiian tan and crisp, casual clothing said *Money*. I walked behind his swivel chair and ambled over to the tape machine.

The closer I got, the more Possum fidgeted. He tried to look cool, standing there in his Florida football jersey, like he was too busy to notice or care what I was doing. He didn't fool me.

"Good to see ya, sweetheart," I said too loudly and too friendly. I slid my arms around his waist, or rather where his waist should be. His torso was one long snaky extension with stick arms and stick legs. Pulling him back toward me, I whispered past the limp hair that hung to his crew collar. "Now, Slick, you ought to know better than to provoke me," I said softly. "You don't want me to get upset and tell every-body about our talk, do you?"

His heels rocked as I held him a little off balance. We're about the same height, but I probably outweighed him. I turned my head toward the girls, both silently begging *No!* with their looks, and gave them a reassuring wink.

Laying my cheek alongside his, I said, "You play nice, and I'll play nice, okay?" I squeezed him tight and planted a juicy kiss on his face before letting him go.

Possum and I'd had a run-in several years ago. Catherine had trained him as an assistant engineer at his first studio job. To show his gratitude, the little pervert flashed her late one night after everyone else had gone home. When she didn't reciprocate, he acted as if she were the bad guy. He started mumbling "bitch" under his breath every time they passed each other. I heard him do it and made Catherine tell me about it.

I waited until he was alone. After locking the control room door behind me, I advanced and cornered him. In a calm voice I explained why he would never, ever do anything like that again.

To his credit, he saw the error of his ways due to the logic of my argument. But whether due to logic or to the little red light that glowed *ready* on the hot curling iron I held, Possum heeded the call of redemption. Assured I had the tools, the talent, and the true desire to use both, we came to an understanding. To my knowledge, he hasn't dropped his drawers since.

The chatter covered my little talk with Possum as Jill and Luanne vied for David's attention. Jill brought the long shank of her blonde hair up with her fingertips and let it all fall behind down her back. While she attempted to get David to talk about his future projects, ones that might include us, Luanne sat next to her, wide-eyed and perky as usual.

After listening to the first song, we made notes on its number chart and went to the studio floor. Around the mike were three wooden stools and three music stands, with a set of headphones on each one.

Jill put her chart on the middle stand while Luanne and I swiveled ours back and down to make tables. I set my water bottle down on mine; Luanne used hers for her diet cola and eyeglasses, which she would only put on at the last minute.

"What's wrong with your face?" she asked me, cocking her headphones off one ear. Jill's eyes scrunched up, looking my way a moment, then she returned to the business of getting set up.

"I slept on it," I said. I knew Luanne would buy this, since one of her favorite beauty secrets to avoid wrinkles is to sleep on your back. My jaw was hardly swollen now. A little extra concealer had covered the blue spot and brightened up the dark circles under my eyes from getting no sleep the past few days.

I decided not to tell the girls about my night in the cemetery. What would I say—*I told you so*?

There was no reason to worry them now, I figured. Besides, with the attitude Jill had been giving me, I really didn't care if they believed me anymore.

Looking through the glass, I watched Possum at the control board on the left and David sitting at the producer's table attached on the right. Talk about complete opposites. Both had graying hair, but on David it made him look distinctive. Possum's just made him look more like a possum.

David leaned into the mike on his table and pressed the talk-back switch. "Ready, ladies?" he said into our headphones. The switch crackled with a loud pop as he released it. He pressed it again, but this time his voice cut in and out, like the button had a bad connection. The tape began and I closed my eyes for a quick meditation to focus on the job at hand.

I had underestimated the soreness of my ribs. As much as I tried to forget the cemetery, my diaphragm reminded me with each breath. I could rest later, I told myself and kept plugging away. Normally I stand through the entire session. This time I took advantage of the stool and tried to pace myself for the duration.

"One more run-through and we're done," David said into the talk-back. The switch popped again while he talked. He pressed it several times as if it were stuck in the ON position. I imagined too many coffee spills and cigarette ashes on the producer's table probably caused it to get sticky and act up. Pressed down, the producer's mike was on, so we heard him and everything going on around him. The button finally released with a click, cutting off the sound of the control room and restoring our own voices in our headsets again.

While the tape rewound, the door behind David and Possum opened. A familiar figure walked in and stood smiling at us from the other side of the glass. It was Hank Tidwell, part owner of Music Max.

He bent his six-foot-plus frame in half, down to the talk-back mike. "Well, if it ain't the singing nuns," he said into it.

The fingers pressing the switch also held a lit cigarette that dropped ashes right into the button as Hank talked. "Y'all are about the prettiest things I've seen in Lord knows how long," he said. As he stood, he let go of the talk-back switch, but it stuck again in the ON position, allowing us to hear the conversation in the control room without their knowledge.

"Yes, sir," Hank said to David and Possum, "those girls are something else."

"They're great," David said. "They do a fantastic job every time."

"Oh yeah, sure. But the main thing is they look good," Hank said.

Jill and Luanne started eyeballing each other, clearly enjoying the compliment.

Hank puffed on his cigarette and said, "Y'all aren't going to believe this. I just had a phone call from my old buddy Jud Sherrill. He said Miss Willi out there has gone completely berserk."

I couldn't believe my ears. Jill and Luanne immediately turned to me.

"She seems fine to me," David said. "What happened?"

"She called the police on him! Said somebody had been trying to kill her at his place out there on the river. I asked him, I said, 'Son, you haven't been screwing around with her on the side, have you?' That's the only explanation I could come up with. I mean, why else do women say crazy things like that?"

David threw his hands up and said, "Who knows. Doesn't sound like Willi, but the female mind is certainly a mystery to me."

"You got that right," Hank said. "Jud wouldn't admit to an affair, but I reckon he was covering for her. Didn't want to drag her name through the mud. I could tell from the way he talked he was being a gentleman and trying to do the honorable thing."

Jill and Luanne were merely shocked. I was completely paralyzed. The three of us stared at each other in disbelief when another voice came over our headphones.

"I believe it." Next to David, Possum's gray mustache twitched above non-existent lips and yellow teeth. "She's a real bitch," he said. "Always has been."

Hank ground out his cigarette while he blew out a stream

of smoke. "You know, you try to help these women out," he said. "You get them work, you're nice to them, and what do you get for your trouble? You get sued, that's what. Sexual harassment, all that. They get their hormones a little bit off kilter and go crazy on you for no reason. Hell, we could be next. I won't be hiring her again."

Hank dropped a heavy hand on David's shoulder and patted it. "I just thought you ought to be warned."

As the door closed behind Hank, the headphones started crackling again. I turned away to look up into the control room where David pressed the talk-back button.

"Can you hear me?" he said, fiddling with the switch until it unstuck.

"Yes," we said together, our voices pitched higher than normal. Luanne was first, beaming up an *Everything's okay* smile to David, then Jill followed, showing all her teeth. I took a deep breath, turned to the control board, and smiled in suit.

"Okay, let's do it," David said, turning to the engineer.

With a purposeful tap to his remote, Possum rolled the tape. He leaned back in his chair, touching the fingers of both hands together in front of his greasy mustache. The music started as he rocked gently backwards, his mouth slowly spreading into a grin.

After the session, Jill, Luanne, and I entered Houston's Restaurant without speaking. The trip to our table, the scanning of menus, and the stretch between ordering drinks and supper were spent in silence. As the waiter zipped our menus away, we looked about the room distractedly, finding it difficult to reconnect after our strange experience at David Payton's session.

Jill finally took off her sunglasses, making a slow trip from her head to the table. Luanne, knowing this was a sign of a rough conversation ahead, popped into her chatterbox mode. It's what she does to make strangers comfortable, flitting from one unrelated topic to another. In a matter of minutes, we heard her jump from the color of the restaurant's curtains to the latest Vanderbilt football tragedy to the pros and cons of breast enlargement, ending up on the subject of Jennalyn Wade.

"I'm sooo excited about going to L.A.," she said. "Before you got to the studio, Willi, David said he was going to be there the same time we are, and that maybe we could get together for dinner one night, isn't that great?"

"Great," I said. "Do we have a definite date for leaving now?"

"Yeah. Jill talked to Jennalyn's office. We go three weeks from next Monday," Luanne said as the two of us looked to our blonde friend. Normally Jill would've given a complete rundown of the situation. Instead, she said nothing.

From her special saucer of extra lemons, she picked up a wedge and squeezed it into her iced tea. After a thorough stirring, she took a sip, patted her mouth with her napkin, and gave me an expectant look.

"Well?" she said finally. "Do we have to sit here all night or are you going to tell us what Hank Tidwell was talking about?"

Before I could take a breath to answer, Luanne jumped in for me and said, "That was a bunch of baloney. Why, the very idea! Willi would never have an affair with Jud Sherrill. It's the most ridiculous thing I've ever heard. He's at least fifty years older than us, right? She's bad off, but not *that* bad. I mean, Willi and Jud? Ha! I don't even want to picture it. What a pack of lies! It's *so* funny." She slapped her thigh and laughed to emphasize just how hilarious it all was, hoping to pull Jill into a lighter mood.

It didn't work. Although her lips curled into a smile, Jill's eyes were cold. "And yet," she said, "when we were at Jud's party the other night, I remember he grabbed your shoulders as we came out of the elevator."

"Oh, for heaven's sake, Jill," I said.

She held a finger in the air and continued, "And then you waited until the rest of us left so you could speak to him. Alone."

I snorted and looked to Luanne for support. She avoided

me, knitting her eyebrows and staring at the ceiling.

Jill folded her arms across her chest. "And what about the way you acted after our session with Jud? You *said* you were looking for somebody who shot at you. Isn't it a strange coincidence that Jud was gone the same time you *said* you were wandering around the building? Y'all were both gone a long time."

"I'm not believing this," I said.

"What about that part where you called the police on him? I suppose there's no truth to that either."

I was so caught up in denying whatever Jill came up with I said, "No, of course not!" without thinking. Somewhere between the "course" and the "not" I realized that wasn't precisely true and amended my answer to, "Well, yes. Not really. Sort of."

I *had* gone to the police. After my meeting with Bracken, he must have gone over to Jud's place to look around. Or shake things up. If that was his intention, he did a good job of it.

Jill shook her head gently from side to side. "I just can't see how you could do this to us," she said.

"What's this 'us' business?" I said, wondering how my being shot at, drugged, abducted, beat up, and left lying in the mud in a cemetery during a typhoon had anything to do with either of them.

A woman sitting across the room waved her arms at me. I looked in her direction. "Willi!" she hollered.

A set of purple chiffon sleeves frantically tried to shush the lady from the other side of her table. Whoever was attached to the arms had taken cover behind a large tropical plant.

"What you do affects us," Jill said. "We've worked too long and too hard to suddenly get stupid and throw it all away. Are you even listening to me?"

"I'm listening," I said. "And I agree. It was thoughtless of me to notify the authorities of my attempted murder without first considering your feelings. I apologize. Now if you'll excuse me, I'm really not very hungry anymore."

As I walked toward the door, I realized the woman still waving at me was Stephanie Schaefer. She wore a straw-colored dress and red sandals. A red carnation bloom was stuck above one ear. Her dinner companion, the plant with arms, sat behind a menu that hid everything but the top of a gray bouffant hairdo.

"I thought that was you," Stephanie said. Her neck fell limply to the side as she said, "Good to see you." With her ear now parallel to the floor, the carnation fell out. Stephanie giggled while scraping her hand around the carpet to retrieve it.

*High again,* I thought, noticing a pungent odor that grew stronger the closer I got to the table. *Wait a minute. That's not pot.* I turned toward the source of the smell, the person behind the menu, and at the same time recognized it as an expensive perfume. As the menu slowly lowered, a pair of no-line designer bifocals appeared. With a quick snap, the menu hit the table and Douglas Anne Pennington's face turned on the charm.

"Why, Willi, what a surprise!" she said. "I didn't know you wuh *hee*-yuh."

"Have a seat," Stephanie said.

"We were just leaving," Doug said as she took her charge card off a little black tray. She pushed her purple sleeves up and twisted in her chair to get her shoulder bag from behind her.

"But you haven't finished your coffee," Stephanie said.

"Stephanie has been telling me," Doug said, "caffeine is bad for you. I believe she's right. Ready, dear?"

*What are they up to?* Doug seemed awfully anxious to get away from me. *Aha!* I thought, realizing Stephanie must be the reason Doug stole the S file from Sam's office. But what was the big secret?

"I was just leaving, too," I said. "May I walk out with you?"

It hit me that Stephanie's number *couldn't* have been the S file Doug wanted. Since she had known Stephanie all of her life, Doug would already have had her number and address.

Once outside, Stephanie turned to me and said, "You look stressed. Your aura is a little orange today. I didn't notice

— 124 —

that before."

I can handle compliments. And I can usually handle insults. But how to properly handle being called "orange" was a new one.

"Hmm," I said.

Stephanie assured me she could fix me up with a potion that would return me to my correct color.

With Douglas Anne on one side of Stephanie and me on the other, we walked to our cars. I was glad I wasn't any closer to Doug. Her perfume was so strong it might have disabled me.

I was wondering how Stephanie could stand it when suddenly an ear-splitting squeal of tires was right behind us. I jumped and glanced back with one movement, seeing a chrome bumper inches away. My scream, undetectable under the high-pitched shriek of tires, lasted only a second. The impact sent me flying headfirst. After landing on my side on a grassy area by the parking lot, I skidded to a stop and rolled over in time to see the rusted rear end of a Torino zoom out of sight.

I shook my head, and tried to sit up. When I did, I saw the red carnation, fallen again, and a small red pool spreading around Stephanie's hair.

Instruments clattered and drawers shut while I stared up from the examination table. The disembodied voice of a nurse said, "You can get dressed now. Stop at the desk before you go—there's a policeman wanting to speak to you." She closed the door behind her, leaving me alone in the cold room.

Once dressed, I walked down the hallway toward the nurses' station. With one arm leaning on the high counter, Detective Bracken spoke quietly to the head nurse. He didn't say anything when he saw me, just motioned with his head toward the waiting area.

"Are you the only cop in Nashville?" I asked, easing down onto a couch.

"Feels like it sometimes."

"How did you know I was here?"

"I have my ways." About the same time he said it, I saw Officer Meadows, the policewoman who had responded to my burglary call. She looked over to us, her sixth sense in good working order. Beside her was a weeping and bedraggled Douglas Anne.

"You okay?" I didn't like the way Bracken said it, like I looked worse than he wanted to let on. He hiked his pants at the knees and sat beside me.

"Just scratched up. No broken bones, thank goodness," I said. A loud honk startled me even though I immediately recognized it. Across the room, Douglas Anne blew her nose and continued talking to Officer Meadows.

"What can you tell me about this afternoon?" Bracken asked me. "Did you get a good look at the driver?"

I shook my head. "All I saw was grill coming at me."

"What about the car?"

"The rear lights looked like an old Gran Torino. I'm not sure, but I think I've seen it before." I told him about Doug's car on River Road.

He looked over to Douglas Anne. One purple sleeve had been cut off, the other rolled up. Both arms were bandaged. Her legs were bare now, with white gauze taped across her shins and knees.

"I'll talk to her," he said finally, then whispered, "Strange."

"Yeah. She's kind of an oddball."

Bracken wheezed out a laugh. "No. I mean, if this was deliberate, which one of you was he going for? This lady," he said, pointing to Doug, "was nearest the street. With her on the end, he could have swerved just a little and taken her out. Yet Ms. Schaefer sustained the worst injuries. Seems strange."

From the look he gave me, I believe he left off the rest of what he was thinking: *Unless he was aiming for you.*

"Couldn't it have been a simple hit and run? Someone lost control of his car, freaked when people were hit, and took off?"

He shrugged. "Anything's possible."

In the hallway directly in front of us, a man in a suit and tie turned the corner. He walked slowly toward us with downcast eyes.

I shifted in my seat, turning my face as much away from him as possible. Douglas Anne jumped up when she saw him and hobbled over in obvious pain.

"I'll be right back," Bracken said. "Sit tight."

*No problem*, I thought. After our last encounter, the last thing I wanted was to speak to Martin Schaefer Jr. again.

I couldn't hear their conversation, but from the shrug of Martin's shoulders I gathered Stephanie still wasn't out of the woods. Doug squeezed and held him a few minutes then began a loud, detailed version of her story while Bracken listened.

When I heard Doug say "Willi," I grabbed a magazine and pretended to be engrossed in an article on colostomies. I cut my eyes above the pages to see Martin staring at me. He headed my way.

"Well, well. We meet again," he said over the magazine.

"Oh, Mr. Schaefer! How's Stephanie?" My voice trembled. I saw his glare soften toward me as I winced trying to stand up. With the pain angle working, I may have exaggerated my condition a bit to keep up the sympathy factor.

"Not good," he said. "She's in the recovery room. The doctor says head injuries are unpredictable, so we'll have to wait and see."

"I'm sorry. You lost your father and now this. I'm sure Stephanie will be fine."

"You seem to have taken quite an interest in her, Ms. Taft," he said as the lawyer in him slowly returned. "I'd be very interested—"

"Darling," Douglas Anne said as she pushed Martin down into the couch, "now you sit down and you re-*lah*-yex. And don't you worry about a thing."

When she put her hand on my back, I braced myself, thinking I was next. Instead, she only patted me and said, "I'm so glad you're all right, dear." Abruptly, she turned her back to me and plopped down where I had been sitting so she could be next to Martin.

"Excuse me," I said. "My friends are here." Thankful for Doug's rescue, I left Martin in her hands and made my way down the hall toward Jill and Luanne.

I gave them the rundown on the doctor's report but didn't mention Bracken's take that the accident wasn't an accident. Still keeping an eye on Doug, Martin, and Bracken, I noticed they kept looking at me. When I lip-read the word "binoculars," my stomach flipped. I decided it might be a good idea to go.

I went to bed early but couldn't fall asleep. Like a tape machine gone berserk, my mind jerked back and forth over the day's events—finding out Jud Sherrill was badmouthing me all over town, arguing with Jill, seeing that car right on my heels.

My brain stopped, started, and stopped again abruptly, reversing and replaying random scenes since Sam's death, then rearranging them into crazy sequences. It was like sitting in a twelve-theater cinema with no walls, like I was in a swivel chair at the center, spinning as all twelve screens alternately flashed explosions, slapstick, bursts of profanity, cartoon violence, screaming women. All swirling together, the pressure melded and condensed into a small, hard mass that ricocheted like a bullet around the inside of my skull.

The black sleep mask over my eyes only intensified the nightmare movie house. With a huff, I slung it off my head and went to the stereo, hoping a CD would soothe me.

My first choice was Rubinstein playing Brahms. I should have known better. Rubinstein is just too brilliant. Even the calmer passages, performed with such beauty and tenderness, threatened their own dark introspection.

Since that was territory I wanted to leave, I put on a collection of Celtic harp instrumentals. After the second number, though, the gentle plinking of the strings felt like being tickled, which can be irritating if you're not in the mood for it.

Next I tried some Baroque a cappella pieces. Usually I love these because they remind me of the good old days of singing in college choral groups. But this record's interlocking voicings were too involved, too taxing on me; at least they were that night.

Inserting another disc, I went down to the next level. I closed my eyes and envisioned myself in a dark hooded robe singing Gregorian chants. This would have worked, I believe, if the phone hadn't rung.

"Hello?" I said, not able to think of a single person I wanted to talk to.

On the other end, the phone receiver fumbled. In the background I heard music and what sounded like a crowded bar. Wondering who was drunk and needing a ride home, I said "hello" again without much enthusiasm.

"Whitewash, where you at?" The voice was one I hadn't heard in ages. The black velvet of it washed over me as I recognized Melvin Jones, a friend I hadn't seen since I left Alabama. "You there?" he said. "That is *you*, isn't it?"

"Melvin, it's been so long I forgot it was me. Nobody's called me that in twenty-five years." I knew Melvin when I was a kid in high school. He drove a truck at the furniture store where my daddy worked. On weekends he played in a band at The Blue Orchid, a black dance club owned by his uncle.

"We're in a club in the middle of downtown—"

"In Nashville?"

"Yeah," he said. "We're set up and fixing to play. I'd planned on calling you anyway to see if you wanted to give us a listen . . ."

"Oh, Melvin, I'd love to but I don't think I'm up to it tonight." I rubbed my bruised calves as if that might win some sympathy when he couldn't even see me.

". . .but right when we were about to leave home, my chink man's wife went into labor and he had to stay down there. That's when I knew I *had* to call in hopes you might want to give an old friend a hand."

*His chink man.* He meant his rhythm guitar player, the one who gives a number texture by playing patterns that sometimes sound like *chink-chink.*

"Aw, jeez. It's not that I don't want to, Melvin. I just don't know if I can do it."

"What's the matter, your axe rusted you ain't played it in so long?"

"No, but my hands are," I said. It had been at least five years since I'd played my guitar in public.

I could hear him laughing into the phone. "Chops come back. It's like riding a bicycle."

"I never did get the hang of that either."

"Quit stalling and come on down here. I know you want to. Come sit in with us just for fun. It wouldn't have taken any convincing in your younger days. Hang on," he said. I could hear somebody ask him something, then Melvin answer, "Yeah, she's coming," before coming back on the line. "We already got your amp set up. All you have to do is plug in. We're at a club called 3rd and Lindsley. Know where that is?"

"Let's see, the corner of 3rd and Lindsley?"

"That's the place. You can hook up with us whenever you get here. See you in a few."

Before I could make excuses, he hung up. I sat there holding the phone, my mouth open. Buddy, the psychic wonderdog, could tell no one was on the other end of the line and dragged himself closer to me. He cocked his head to the side and smacked his lips up and down. This was his way of saying, "Keep talking, friend. I'll listen to you."

With a click I put the phone down. I rubbed Buddy's head and said, "Sweetheart, I'm going out."

Dark ribbons of clouds flew ahead of me as I drove down Broadway. The full moon, flat and shiny as a silver dollar, shone beside the Gothic stone clock tower of Union Station, Nashville's old railroad depot, and glinted over the rust of its dilapidated train sheds.

The eeriness of the picture reminded me of an old movie scene. An English gentleman rode his horse across the moors, screaming in the moonlight, riding all night through early morning. He'd spur the horse on, faster and faster in order to relieve the pain from a brain tumor. The speed, pressing against the cold night wind, was his only sedative. At dawn, the horse ambled home, carrying his master, who now lay exhausted across the mane, finally able to sleep.

Remembering the numbness that can come from dark bars and too-loud music, I hoped my own night ride would produce similar results. I pressed the accelerator and sped down Broadway toward the club and the moon.

Although I parked a good way from the building, I could hear the thumping of the drums and bass down the street. The familiar sounds sent a wave of jitters from my stomach up over my chest. I took a deep breath and grabbed my case out of the trunk.

Before leaving the house, I put new strings on my guitar, a black Stratocaster, and took a quick trip to the woodshed, practicing scales and chords to limber up my fingers. When they were good and tingly, I put on a black shirt and black pants to make myself as inconspicuous as possible, and determined to hide all night behind Melvin on stage.

Playing guitar had been a big part of my life during my first few years in Nashville. I played in a little blues band that worked three nights a week, but it had been years since I'd played in front of anyone. Unless you count Buddy. He always sits with me when I play at home. I took a deep breath and squared my shoulders as I approached the club's front door.

The place was packed. I shoved through to the back of the main room and leaned my case against the bar. Only about half the customers were lucky enough to have a seat. The other fifty percent stood squashed against each other in aisles and three or four deep along the walls.

Glancing over this crowd, I could tell it was an extra good one. It was Saturday night. Everyone facing the stage moved in some way to the groove being laid down by Melvin and his band, Blues Jones. When he announced a break, I made my way to the stage to get set up.

"Relax," Melvin said after I met the band. "It's no big thing. We're gonna do all the work. All you have to do is enjoy the ride."

Standing over me, the band members laughed while I ran a polish cloth over my guitar. Their dark faces had a sheen of sweat, both shining and shadowed with their backs turned to the stage spots on the floor. I laughed from way inside, the first time in too long of a time. Seeing them there, I felt a deep sigh in my body. *These are good people, my own people. Home folks. Here to bring me back to myself, willing to carry me through a rough night.*

If it wouldn't have made me look like a fool, I'd have reached up, hugged their necks, and cried into their shirts. Instead I held my guitar up tight against me and said, "I'll do my best to keep up."

Just before we started the set, a waitress came by with a tray of cold beers for us. I took a big swig and set my bottle down out of the way behind my case.

And then we played. By the time beer two came around, my hands were feeling right. It felt good. Melvin spoke the truth—they did the hard work, and all I had to do was fall back until I was lost in the notes, until my part was so natural and automatic it seemed like someone else was playing it.

The blare of the speakers formed a wall around us. From the middle of it, Melvin's guitar set about its soothing work. *Yes, ma'am, the doctor is in.*

*That was it,* I thought. This was what I'd needed earlier when I went through my CDs. That single line of a blues solo, that distilled crying was the plainsong I needed. Not in the quiet chants at Vespers, but in loud, soulful lamentations in the midnight hour.

Once, in between songs, Melvin turned to me. He nodded toward the swinging door behind the bar where bright light spilled in from the kitchen. It was propped open by a little white lady wearing a white apron and cap. She smiled at us and applauded with the rest of the audience.

"Hey, that remind you of anything?" he asked over the noise. He rubbed a hand towel around his face then shook the rag toward the door.

"No, sir," I said. "I ain't doing no dishes this time around."

"What a sight you were, Whitewash. What a sight!" While we had a laugh, the rest of the band saw the cook in the door. I could tell from their expressions they'd already heard the story of how Melvin and I became friends.

On my fifteenth birthday, Daddy told me to come after school to the store where he worked, and he would give me my present. It was a Silvertone, an electric guitar he bought at a pawn shop down the street. I already had a beat-up three-quarter size guitar that I learned to play on, but the Silvertone was a real instrument, at least in my eyes.

I was ecstatic. I ran out to the loading dock at the back of the furniture store with the Silvertone strapped on tight. A radio was usually on out there where the delivery guys hung out, and I sat next to it playing along with the hits until time for the store to close. Melvin was there, and I remember he asked if I had a record player. I said I did, and he said, "If I bring you a record, can you play what's on there?" I said sometimes I could.

The next time I went to the store, he had some old blues albums for me to listen to. I studied and practiced them every day like I was going to be tested. When I had done all I could and returned them, Melvin helped me with chords I couldn't figure out and gave me pointers about playing lead.

"I wish there was someplace around here you could play this kind of music," I said to him. "Or at least just listen." He and the other deliverymen, all black, threw back their heads and laughed at such a naive comment.

"Suppose I told you there *was* such a place, where people listened to rhythm and blues, danced all night, and actually had a good time—right here in this town. Would you believe me?" Melvin's eyes twinkled, amused I'm sure at my astonished look.

One of the other guys on the dock said, "No use in telling her since she can't go down there." They were talking about The Blue Orchid.

Of course, that was all the dare it took for a headstrong teenager like me. All I wanted to do was listen, but there were obstacles, big ones, to keep me from going to The Blue

Orchid. My mama, for one. She would never have agreed to let me go to a black club late at night by myself.

That's why I didn't tell her. My daddy lived across town, and at the time, I stayed with him on Friday nights. Since the two of them never talked or saw each other, all I had to do was tell Mama I was at Daddy's, and tell Daddy I'd be at his house late.

The biggest problem was convincing Melvin's uncle, the owner of the club, to let me come in. It was a private club, one where members brought their own brown bag, with no minors allowed. He said his customers didn't want to see any white folks when they came in his place, because that's why they were there—to forget about us.

The only way I managed to convince him was I agreed to wash dishes. I told him I'd stay in the kitchen where nobody would see me, and work in an apron and hat. He allowed it on the conditions that I only come on Friday, since the crowd was smaller than Saturday night, and that I go home after the first set.

My second week on the job, Melvin came into the kitchen before the band started. He had a folding chair under one arm and held the end of a long guitar cord in his hand. His uncle looked at me, I looked at Melvin, and Melvin looked back at both of us.

"You didn't say she couldn't play from the kitchen." He opened the chair up, slapped it down behind the door, and said, "You *did* bring your guitar, didn't you?"

I was out the back screen before either of them could say anything, and inside again with my Silvertone before Melvin could change his mind. From then on, I was constantly waiting for Friday night, when I played my heart out amid the clatter of dishes and the smell of fine barbecue.

One night while I was sitting there playing, the back door opened and in walked my daddy. He'd known all along. He and Melvin's uncle stood there laughing at me, and I knew then why I'd really been allowed to be there. The furniture store where Daddy worked was the only one in town that would do business with folks in the black community. Everybody, including Melvin's uncle, knew my daddy better than I did, knew what a good man he was, and that's why he let me play.

After buying a pigskin, Daddy came over to my chair and kissed me on the forehead. "Don't you never tell your mama," he said. "She'll kill us both." He shook hands with the cook and winked at me before going out the screen door.

Later on, during my junior and senior years of high school, I played all night, Fridays and Saturdays, but still washed dishes between sets, always in my cap and apron, and always playing from the kitchen.

*Whitewash.* I looked over at Melvin, who had hardly aged a bit the last twenty-five years. Beer number three came around but I only took a sip. One and two had already done their trick, making me teary-eyed and nostalgic.

With only candlelight to see the audience, it was easy to overlay memories of home like a transparency over the room. The darkness and the heat made it seem like a summer night in Alabama. The back bar looked like a porch, a lot like the porch of the crazy old man with a cane who Douglas Anne met the day I followed her. As the bartender switched a keg, I remembered the barrel next to the old man that smelled and bubbled up a dark brew.

*Dark brew.* A waitress set a stout porter on a table nearby. I nearly died looking over to the large beer pull with the unmistakable logo of Ireland's most famous beer.

*Guiness*, I thought as I made the connection. *I've caught you, you rascal.*

On the way home, I was still so charged up from playing I didn't realize I was being followed until I was all the way home. As I was about to turn into my driveway, the headlights split in two. For a moment, I thought it was a couple of UFOs circling. Then I realized I hadn't been followed by aliens, but by two motorcycles. It wasn't much of a relief.

# CHAPTER 12

THE INSTANT I WOKE UP I was ready to jump out of bed. You'd think after the rough day and late night I'd had, I'd be copping serious *zzz*'s on Sunday morning. But I had a mission—to find out just who "Guiness" was and why he'd been bugging me with those insane faxes.

I laughed, thinking how they had shaken me. Knowing they were sent by an old crippled guy instead of a psycho was some comfort. If he *were* able to sneak up on me (doubt it), he wouldn't be able to catch me. If he caught me, he wouldn't be able to do much damage.

On the other hand, if Guiness was only a nuisance and not a physical threat, who had been trying to kill me?

At 7:30 A.M., I drove up the gravel incline toward Guiness's house. Before I'd gone hardly a quarter of the way onto his property, a gray-and-black-dappled collie dashed toward the car. He escorted me up, barking and running from side to side as if I were a brainless sheep who needed herding.

The old man was waiting for me on the back porch. "Good boy," I heard him call. The collie gave a final bark, of warning or welcome I wasn't sure, before turning his back and trotting over to his master's side.

The old man's dentures flashed as I walked toward him. This was a relief since I'd figured he might not be too thrilled to see an uninvited guest so early in the morning.

"What took you so long?" he asked. "Come on in. I've been expecting you. Jake Stoner," he said, stretching out his hand.

Before I could tell him my own name, he pivoted with the help of his cane and opened the screen door for me. "How about some coffee? I've got a fresh pot."

"Sure. Thanks," I said and stepped ahead of him into his

kitchen. "Mr. Stoner, I'm—"

"So you're the famous Willi." Hobbling over to the counter, he took a mug down out of an overhead cabinet. The kitchen was typical of a sixties ranch-style—dark wood paneling, black wrought-iron pulls and hinges on the drawers and cabinets, a hanging wagon-wheel light only a man could love.

He brought my cup over to the table and motioned for me to have a seat. "Sam told me all about you," he said. His voice rasped as he leaned down into his chair. To his right was an oxygen tank on wheels. He rolled it closer and took a hit.

"Funny, he never mentioned you." I took a sip and, hearing a bumping noise at the door, turned to see the collie outside against the screen. He gave me a look over his shoulder, then settled with his thick fur sticking in through the mesh.

"Good," he said. "I'm a secret." He set the plastic mouthpiece on the table and gave me a mischievous smile. "I could tell you why, but I'd have to kill you."

"Very funny. Mr. Stoner, if you don't start some explaining, I might have to kill *you*."

"It's Jake, and it would be harder to do than you think." He scrunched the sleeve of his polo shirt up under his armpit, turned his fist inward, and flexed his biceps. "I'm lean and I'm mean," he said, laughing, then immediately had a hacking fit. He drank about half a glass of water and got up to refill it at the sink.

"You sure you're okay?" I said after he recovered.

He nodded and sat back down. "It took you long enough to find me. Didn't you get my messages? I was about to give up on you."

"I'm here, aren't I? And those weren't messages, they were annoyances. A message is a clear, understandable communication. Your little notes were not only cryptic, they were downright aggravating."

He wheezed out a laugh and said, "I was testing your detecting skills."

*Test this*, I thought, but didn't say it since I lacked the equipment to make the proper accompanying gesture.

"Some detective," he said. "You found me three days ago and didn't even know it. You squealed out of here just as I realized who you were. When I recognized Sam's car I tried to stop you but you kept going."

"Sorry, but at the time my mind was on that thief, Douglas Anne Pennington."

"Thief?"

I told him that Doug had stolen the S cards from Sam's address file. "So you were the reason for that," I said. "At least that's one thing out of this whole mess that's cleared up. Why did she come to see you? Or is that classified information?"

"Ah, she's crazy. She wanted me to confirm some wild suspicions about a mutual friend of ours." He paused a moment to take a sip of coffee and sat there looking at me. "You know that funeral you and Sam went to? For Martin Schaefer? He was the friend."

"We saw Mrs. Pennington there. She wasn't very complimentary of the deceased."

"I don't expect she was. She hated him. It was his wife, Lucy, who was her friend. That's what she wanted to talk to me about. Douglas Anne has decided, after thinking about it for some twenty-odd years, that Lucy was abused. That her husband was a wife-beater."

"Why did she think you would know?" I asked.

"How about a warm up?" Jake rose slowly and limped over to the coffeemaker. With his back to me, he said, "Because Martin was my partner."

"A business partner?"

"No. My partner on the police force. For eleven years. I guess Douglas Anne figured if anyone knew Martin Schaefer, it would be me."

"But you weren't at his funeral." I said it before thinking. My eyes traveled over to the oxygen tank.

"Let's just say Martin and I weren't exactly on speaking terms." We sat drinking our coffee while Jake seemed caught up in whatever past disagreement he had with his old partner.

"So you don't buy what Douglas Anne said—that Martin was the type to hit his wife?"

"No, of course not. I'd have known if he was. Doug has too much time to think and not enough brains to think with. She's nothing but a rich dingbat."

"Speaking of dings, what did you make of somebody trying to run her off the road that day she came to see you?" I asked.

"She said it was just a redneck trying to pass her on the two-lane."

"If she said that, she *is* a dingbat. You saw how dented up that Cadillac was. It was done on purpose."

"People always speed and drive like maniacs on this road."

"Jake, I'm telling you he wanted her off in the ditch. I was behind him, I saw the whole thing."

"Did you get the tag number?"

"No. I'm not sure, but I think I saw the car again. I only got a glimpse of it, but I think it's the same one that came after me, Douglas Anne, and Stephanie Schaefer."

"Marty's girl? Back up. Tell me what happened."

I related the hit-and-run incident and told him Stephanie was still in serious condition.

Jake looked worried. "If it's the same guy, he was going after Doug but got Stephanie instead? Who would want to kill Doug?"

"Don't know," I replied. "The only person I know of would be her ex-husband. She claims he's been breaking into her house and messing things up."

"Hmm. Poor Steph. Luckily you're still in one piece. At least you know he wasn't after you, right?"

I didn't answer.

"Right?" he asked again.

"Well . . . ." I couldn't help it. I needed to talk to someone about all that had happened over the last few days. Jake seemed to fit the bill. The more I told him, the more worried he looked.

"I see why you suspected me. You thought that fax I

sent—'You were too out of it' and 'Next time I keep the car'—meant *I* drove you to the cemetery and beat you up," he said. "I'm sorry. I was only making a joke because I've always loved Sam's car. But why *didn't* he take it? I would have. It's worth a lot of money." I could see the cogs working behind his eyes as he stared off into space. He began nodding, as if carrying on a conversation with himself.

"Amateur," he said. "Not used to thinking like a criminal. Probably no connections in the stolen car market." He thought another minute or so and said, "You want my professional opinion? Somebody's just trying to scare you. He has had at least two golden opportunities to kill you but didn't."

"But why would anyone do that to me? All Sam's cases were either boring or closed as far as I can tell. The only mysterious ones were those I found in his bathroom stash with your name on them. That's another reason you were my prime suspect."

He laughed so hard he had a hacking fit. After downing the water left in his glass, he said "Jake Stoner, Public Enemy Number One."

"But that first fax you sent me—'You were there 7-25-78.' How did you know about Jennalyn Wade's session? I thought surely that meant you were one of my attackers and you had known me from being in the music business yourself."

"That was for Sam, not you. He wanted me to find out a particular date for a case he was starting on."

"Oh." We sat quietly sipping coffee together while I looked around the kitchen. "You keep your place looking nice," I said, noticing the waxed floor and a hint of pine cleaner. "You live alone?"

"Just us two bachelors." He cricked his neck toward the door. "Me and Guiness."

"I don't get it. What do you and the dog have to do with Sam's tapes?"

"That's what I wanted to talk to you about. Sam worked for me. He was going to tell you, but I guess he didn't have the chance. Anyway, I have a few projects for you. To start with, I need you to do some surveillance. The first job is easy—"

"Whoa! I can't just step into Sam's shoes!"

"Why not? Somebody's got to do it."

"Yeah. Somebody else. I'm wrapping up his paperwork. That's it."

"All I want you to do is watch a few people."

"You'd have to tell me about your problems first."

Jake looked up from his cup. "Me? I don't have any."

"Don't give me that. You want to hire a detective—you must have problems. So spill it."

"I thought you didn't want new business," he said. "If you do, you need to work on your interpersonal skills."

I let that one slide and said, "Look. The only reason I came here was to get some answers, like why you were sending me weird faxes, and why Sam hid your files in the wall, and why the police are interested."

Jake's coffee cup stopped in midair. "What makes you think the police are interested?" His face lost its smirk.

I told him that Bracken asked me if I'd ever heard the name *Guiness.* Jake got up and walked over to the sink. He stared out the window a long time before shaking his head. "He was just fishing."

"Looks like he was in the right pond. He's sharp."

"Damn right, he's sharp. I trained him." Jake brought the carafe over and refilled our cups. I gave him the silent treatment, hoping he would feel compelled to talk. When he sat down again he took a deep drag from the oxygen tank.

"So Sam was extra careful," he said, smiling as he thought of him. "I knew he wouldn't leave much of a trail to me."

"*Much?* How about *none?* If Douglas Anne hadn't stolen Sam's file and I hadn't followed her to get it back, I'd never have found you."

"It was completely by accident? No, I don't believe it. You're lucky. Luck is something every good investigator has, and you've got it. You'd have found me one way or the other."

Jake sighed and rested his elbows on the table. "Willi, I

need your help. What I'm about to tell you is strictly confidential, understand?"

"Yes. Of course."

"Because nothing can get back to Metro." His lips tightened as he stressed each word. "Are you with me?"

"I promise, I promise. Now what is it?"

He picked up his mug, blew over the top of it, and took a big slurp. "I play a game," he said in a softer voice. "I work on cases the police department never solved."

My eyebrows went up. "And how do you do this? You don't have access to police records. You said you didn't want the cops on to you, so I take it they aren't aware of your 'game.' Surely you'd let them know if you solved a crime, wouldn't you?"

"I *have* solved crimes. Five, to be exact, in the last few years. And of course I let them know. Anonymously."

"Uh-huh." I let that hang in the air while I stared at him. "Anonymously. Of course."

"You don't believe me."

"I believe you."

"What do you think, I'm making it up? Did I make up those tapes you found?"

"I believe you, already. It's just hard to imagine one guy outsmarting an entire police force. I mean, here you are out in the middle of nowhere, alone; they, on the other hand, are at Info Central with around-the-clock manpower."

He started laughing. He straightened up from his chair and walked past me to an old pie safe. "Don't get me wrong. I miss work. But being alone in the sticks has advantages over that noisy rat maze downtown. Out here, you can think."

He opened the doors on the safe. Stepping back so I could see its contents, he said, "Behold, Info Central."

Inside, instead of pies, the old pine shelves held a computer system and a police scanner.

"Not bad for an old crip, is it?" he said. "As far as the manpower part of your argument is concerned, I had Sam for a leg man. He was perfect. We worked together well when we were partners on the force—"

"Wait a minute! You told me Martin Schaefer was your partner."

"He was. But we sort of had a falling out. He got promoted, and then Sam was my partner for a year or so when he was a rookie. So we knew each other well. And between the two of us, we've solved some old cases."

"This is all incredible. You tip them off and they follow up?"

"Right."

"And you're sure they don't know it's you?"

"Not a clue," he said. "They'd have sent someone over to have a little talk with me if they did. That was the great thing about Sam. He studied electronics and communications in the Navy. He could rig anything with wires to do just about whatever he wanted. He custom designed this," he said, patting a metal box that was identical to the fax machine in Sam's office.

I wiggled my finger in the air. "That's how Bracken made the connection. He saw a fax from you in the office. He would've noticed similarities between it and the ones you sent to Metro."

Jake nodded. "You're right. But he still doesn't know it's me." His chest was starting to rattle. "So what do you think?" he wheezed out before putting the mask on his nose. "Are you interested in doing some detective work?"

I thought a minute. "No. I mean I'm not interested in it as a living. But because you were close to Sam, I'll help you. If I can. Sam would've wanted me to. Whatever he started for you, I'll help finish. But that's all. You'll have to hire a real detective to help you later on. Deal?"

"That's a deal, partner. And you *can* help on this one. It may lead us to Sam's killer."

I turned away and walked over to the screen door. "Now *you're* the one doing the fishing," I said. "Don't kid yourself. You miss Sam and you want to create some nonexistent case, something solvable, in order to make sense of his death. Uncle Ralph and Bracken were right. Sam walked in on a robbery. It's that simple. There's no sense to be made of it."

Jake grunted. "Believe what you want. We're all he's got, you and me. If Bracken had any evidence, there'd have been an arrest by now."

"If *they* can't find anything, how can *I*?"

"You have to. Sam told me he was on to something the afternoon he was killed. He wouldn't tell me what. You've got to try to remember something, anything he might have said about it."

I stood looking through the screen door out over Jake's property. It stretched out in a long downward slope to the edge of some woods, mostly cedars and scrub pines. High above them, two buzzards with huge wingspans floated in circles on a thermal.

"He was crazy about you. He used to stand right where you are and look out, just like that. He talked about buying that land one day, so we could be neighbors. He had everything going for him. His business was doing good, everybody liked him."

I could hear Jake's knees cracking as he got up. "Willi, I don't know what your plans are. Believe me, I understand if you want to close up Sam's office and forget it all. But if you have any interest in his work, I'll be right here. I'll do whatever I can to help out."

I bit my lip, trying not to cry. "No," I said. "I'll bring those tapes over. Maybe you'll hear something in them I didn't. But that's the end of it for me."

Guiness barked as he escorted me down the drive from Jake's house. I'd promised to look over Sam's office and apartment once more, although I trusted the police had done a thorough job. I felt sure I'd have noticed anything unusual as much as I'd shuffled papers around while packing. However, at the time I hadn't known about Jake or his suspicions that Sam's death wasn't a random crime, but murder.

I didn't completely buy it yet, although it explained the attempts on me. Why didn't they just kill me too? *What were you up to, Sam?*

I locked the door behind me as I entered the dim foyer. No lights were on. Enough light from the windows facing Charlotte Avenue came in so that I could see my way to the stairs. I paused a second, looking into the empty pawn shop as I went by.

I could see white through the holes in Sam's mailbox mounted on the paneling. Grabbing the envelopes with one hand and the stair rail with the other, I headed up to the office.

After flipping by a sweepstakes entry, a pizza coupon, and a bill, I stopped on a postcard addressed to Sam. Its computer-printed message said:

*Mr. Robbins,*

*Have you forgotten us? The prints you ordered on July 20th are ready for pick-up. Please come by at your earliest convenience.*

*Thank you for using Waldo's Photo Shop.*

My legs were ahead of my brain. By the time I finished reading the return address, I was already running toward the back door again. According to the postcard, Sam dropped off something to be developed on the day he was killed.

It wasn't until I was standing in line for the pictures that I realized how odd it was for Sam to bring film here. Upstairs, above his apartment, he had a darkroom set up to develop his own negatives. What was so special about these?

When the lady behind the counter handed me the packet, I resisted the urge to rip it open on the spot. The envelope was too thin to contain an entire roll of film, and too big for the usual three-by-fives. The receipt snapped in two as I snatched it from the cashier's fingers and sprinted through the automatic doors.

Once settled in the car, I took a sip of iced tea and tried to calm down. With the air-conditioning on full blast, I pointed the vents toward my face and tore off the top flap of the envelope.

Only two pictures were inside. The photographs were blown up from tiny originals, also enclosed. So that was why

Sam brought them here. His darkroom had only basic developing equipment. The date "May 1978" was typed in red in the margins of each original. In both, the subjects were the same—about twenty teenagers and a few adults. In the first, they waved to the camera from the tables of a sidewalk cafe. In the second one, the kids—all lanky arms and braces—posed around a park bench at the foot of the Eiffel Tower.

I don't know what I expected, but this wasn't it. "This is nothing," I said and slung them on the passenger's seat. On the way to the drugstore, I'd been hoping that this would be the answer, that there'd be a big finger pointing to a menacing bad guy, something clean and straightforward to make sense of it all. I grabbed my cell phone, hoping Jake would have some ideas.

*Wait a minute.* One of Sam's interviews on tape mentioned Paris. Something about a school trip. He interviewed a teacher, maybe one of the adults in the photos. I hung up the phone before I'd finished dialing and drove back to the office.

I got on my knees and grabbed the giant screwdriver from under the sink. With the bathroom heater pried open, I fished out the cassettes again.

The one I wanted was the last one according to its date, July 18th. I listened to the tape all the way through, then played it again.

Mrs. Frazier, the speaker, had been a French teacher at Hillwood High School. From her voice, I tried to match her with one of the adults in the pictures. If I was right, she was the short lady with dark hair and eyes.

The interview was not a strict one. Mostly Sam made small talk, speaking in generalities to put her at ease. Much of the time, the only sound was of pages flipping as the two of them looked through photo albums. They talked of the few summers before and after it, but Sam guided their conversation back to this one, 1978, and to this group. Before the end, Sam asked if she would mind if he borrowed two photos.

"Not at all, Mr. Robbins," Mrs. Frazier said. "It's curious something so long ago would be relevant to a current case. Or perhaps you work on an old one."

I detected a laugh in her voice, as if she knew very well what he was doing but waited for him to tell her himself.

Sam laughed. "You're a sharp lady. I'm probably not the first to ask you about this particular year."

"No, not the first to ask. But the first to be so charming."

Sam didn't reply as she paused, but let the long silence encourage her to speak.

"Casey was a lovely girl," she said finally. "She wasn't the smartest in her class, but she was a good student. That's her mother standing next to me. I never had a problem finding chaperones for a trip."

She paused again as the sound of the album's transparent pages rippled in the microphone. "The police spoke with all her teachers when it happened. I don't think we were much help."

"I won't keep these long," Sam said. "Would you mind writing down the names of everyone in them?"

"I'll do my best. After twenty years, some may have slipped my mind." Mrs. Frazier walked away from the microphone, then came back offering Sam her copy of the school yearbook as a reference for the students she couldn't recall. Sam thanked her and cut off the tape.

I called Jake with the news of my discovery.

"When did you say those pictures were taken?" he asked.

"May of 1978. They kept mentioning a girl that died, Casey somebody."

"Dear God," he said. "Casey Lanham. She was murdered in July of that year. It's one of the biggest unsolved cases in Nashville's history."

I spread the two photos out in front of me. "Which one is she? What did she look like?" I asked.

"Tall, blonde . . . ."

There were three light-haired girls in both pictures. In each, two of them were arm in arm. Suddenly the face of one of the companions jumped off the page at me.

"Jeez!" I yelled. "Is this Stephanie Schaefer?"

"Stephanie and Casey were best friends," Jake said.

"Casey should be close by."

They could've been sisters. The same height, same hair-style, same coloring, and same clothes from their earrings down to their shoes. I remembered her name now. I'd seen it on the microfiche at the library.

When we hung up, I stared at the pictures as the tape played again. I stopped it at the mention of the school annual Sam borrowed. It should still be here in the apartment some-where.

I found it on the bottom shelf of a bookcase. A piece of paper stuck out near the back. It marked the page where the French Club posed on the front steps of Hillwood High.

The paper was the one Mrs. Frazier had written on to go with the two photos. She had remembered most of the stu-dents with only a few question marks instead of names. Over the spaces she left blank, Sam had penciled in names, ones I presumed he'd matched using the yearbook.

The last thing I expected was to see the name of some-one I knew. Since I had not grown up here, I didn't know many native Nashvillians. Almost all the people I knew in the music business were like me, from somewhere else.

Mrs. Frazier had not forgotten this student. With his high-profile father and his own work garnering several gold records, the teacher had no trouble remembering the dark-haired junior in the shadow of the Eiffel Tower—Blaine Sher-rill, Jud Sherrill's son.

Mrs. Frazier had not heard about Sam's death. She told me it was fine for me to come by that afternoon to return the things Sam borrowed.

"Do come in," Mrs. Frazier said as she opened the door to her apartment. "I'm so glad to meet you." She motioned for me to sit on a beautiful antique sofa of rose velour, then perched beside me.

"Would you like a cup of tea?" she asked, not waiting for my answer before she poured. I accepted a cup as fragile as an eggshell. It went well with the rest of the room, a mixture of beautiful old and modern furnishings, all decidedly European.

We chatted about her trips to Paris, before her retirement and since, eventually coming to the one Sam had been interested in. She moved the tea tray aside and opened a large photo album on the table in front of me.

"So you have an interest in the death of Casey Lanham?" she said.

"I'm afraid I've only heard a little about it."

"You must not have been living here at the time. It was all anyone talked about for months."

"You're right. I moved up later," I said and took a sip of tea.

"Of course, crimes are committed everywhere these days, but at the time, it was quite sensational."

"What happened exactly?"

"She disappeared. A few months after our return from Paris, still summer break. She was last seen riding her bicycle near her house in West Meade. Two days later she was found in the woods in Edwin Warner Park, a few miles away. Raped and strangled," she said in a low whisper.

"And there were no suspects?"

"None. No one saw her or anyone else in that area at that time."

I pointed to one of the pictures and said, "I know Stephanie Schaefer. They look very close."

"Oh, yes. Inseparable. Poor Stephanie was devastated."

How happy they looked. The two young girls, oblivious to the horror ahead, leaned on one another as they laughed across the years into the camera. With one arm around the other's shoulder, they stood cheek to cheek, holding out identical necklaces, their hair styled the same, showing the bond closer than twins—they were best friends.

"What about her bicycle? Had it been abandoned somewhere?"

"No, it was beside her. She liked the park and rode the trails often. It was assumed she went alone and was lured off the path by her attacker."

I turned the page. Most of the pictures there were of the adults. On the last page, the chaperones stood together on the banks of the Seine in front of a barge.

My hand shot out and pointed at the face of one of the ladies. "What!" I yelled. "It can't be!"

Mrs. Frazier leaned over the table to see. "That's Douglas Anne Pennington," she said. "You know Doug?"

I was speechless. I nodded.

"What a character," Mrs. Frazier said, chuckling. "She went with our group several times. Mind you, she had no children in my classes. It was just her idea of charity work. She could shop while doing community service."

I looked closer at the photos. Only the nose gave her away. It was no wonder I hadn't recognized her sooner. Her hair was dark in a straight shoulder-length style, quite a contrast to her gray bouffant now. She was also a few dress sizes smaller and was not wearing her trademark bifocals.

"In fact," Mrs. Frazier said, "I believe Stephanie was the reason she became involved. I never knew for sure, but I remember thinking at the time that Doug must have paid Stephanie's way to Paris. Stephanie's mother passed away earlier that year. I think Doug thought the trip might help her."

"I see," I said. "With all that—losing her mother then her best friend not long afterwards—I can see how Stephanie could turn out . . . well, the way she has."

Mrs. Frazier looked away. "Yes," she said slowly, "I understand what you mean. And those things did increase her anxiety. But the truth is she was an overly sensitive girl long before her mother's death."

I wasn't sure how Sam got on this case after so many years. All I knew was there were too many coincidences all of a sudden, too many accidents and break-ins and tie-ins that didn't quite fit together right for me to just drop it all.

"Drop it, bitch." It was a real note left by a real person. Someone had lived with a crime for twenty years. And when I found out who it was, I'd do exactly what I was asked to do. *Drop it. Right on the killer's head.*

Later that night, the phone rang while Buddy and I sat in the floor sorting magazines to recycle. Neither of us felt like getting up. We let the machine speak and listened to the caller leaving a message.

"Hey, Willi, it's Lu," Luanne said, her voice quivering. "About those sessions tomorrow? Forget about them. They've been canceled. Well, *they* haven't been canceled, you're just not . . . I mean, they're not going to need you after all. That's for both of them . . . either of them . . . um, I'll talk to you later." Click.

*What?* Those were master sessions, ones that had been scheduled for months. I got up and replayed the message to be sure I'd heard right, and then I called her back. My hand shook as I pushed in her numbers. Although we weren't supposed to work for Jud Sherrill himself, the sessions were booked at his studio complex with another producer.

When she answered, I said "Luanne, what is this crap you left on my machine? Are you sure about those sessions? It's awfully short notice."

"Yeah, I'm sure," she said softly.

"You said they weren't going to need *me*. Does this mean you and Jill are still doing them?"

"Willi, I'm sorry. I guess they only need two of us," she said, sounding like she was about to cry.

"That's fine. That's fine then," I said, trying to sound controlled and nonchalant. "Whatever."

I could hear the receiver on the other end being moved around, then someone else spoke. "Don't yell at her, Willi. It's not her fault," Jill said in a bitchy tone.

"I wasn't yelling. I was merely trying to get a clear picture of what's going on."

"Okay, picture this: A producer moves here from L.A. He has connections. He has budgets big enough to use background singers. He has lots of projects lined up. And guess what? He's an old friend of ours which puts us in a good position to make some money."

I snorted. "What has Rick Crawford got to do with tomorrow's sessions? I thought we were working for Tom."

"Tom and Rick are both doing projects for SFI Records. They've been working in the same studio for the past few weeks. They play golf together. They talk."

"So? What have I ever done to Rick?"

"It's what you didn't do. I tried to get you to be nicer to him at that party. You hardly spoke! You treated him like the scum of the earth."

"I did not."

"You didn't even try to be nice," she said.

"You mean I didn't giggle and rub up and down his arm enough. How could I? With you and Luanne all over him, there wasn't a square inch available if I'd *wanted* to touch him. Besides, he hired me after that party. *Me*. By myself," I said, remembering that long night with his tone-deaf girlfriend.

The phone was silent. Finally Jill said, "You want to know all of it? Okay, I'll tell you. That stuff we overheard Hank say about you being unstable? Rick knew about it. He also said he already heard you and Jud had been secretly fooling around for a long time."

"You know that's not true," I said. "How do you know Rick said that anyway?"

"Tom's production assistant told Luanne. He overheard Rick, Tom, and Possum. They were not complimentary of you."

"Possum hates me," I said quietly.

"Well, whose fault is that? He's engineering those sessions tomorrow. As far as I'm concerned, you've cooked your own goose."

We sat without talking until I finally said "Bye" and hung up. *Who cares*, I thought. So I missed out on one day of work. It wasn't the end of the world.

# CHAPTER 13

AS I DRANK MY COFFEE the next morning, I stared at the two
reprints of Mrs. Frazier's pictures of Paris. I'd slept in, since
my sessions had been canceled. It was almost ten o'clock.
They'd soon be starting without me.

Buddy put his front paws up on my lap. He looked over
at the clock and did a half-woof/half-snort. I took this to be
his commentary on the situation, roughly translated from
doggie language as *To hell with them and their stupid sessions.*

I kissed him on the nose. "Want to go for a ride?" I asked,
holding his fuzzy yellow ears out to the side. He smiled,
pushed off from my lap, and trotted out of the kitchen. I
knew he would wait by the front door, cleaning the floor with
his wagging tail until I was ready to go.

I decided to cruise by Ju-Ju's to see if Catherine was
working. Turning off the Square, I went down the side street
where the refurbished bungalow stood. Her car was in the lot
so I pulled in, put Buddy on his leash, and the two of us went
in for a visit.

We made our way back to the studio. Catherine had on
her usual T-shirt and faded blue jeans. Her shock of frizzy
red hair bushed out around her face. When she turned to see
who had come in, her features relaxed into a smile. She
raised her arms in a stretch and tapped the STOP button on
the tape machine's remote.

"Mind if we come in?" I asked.

"Not a bit," she replied. "My ears need a break."

While she petted Buddy, I told her about the cancellation
of my work for the day and how frustrated I was getting.

"I heard," she said. "Luanne called me last night."

"You know, I thought I was under control but this mess

is getting to me. My blood pressure is so high my head feels like it's about to explode."

Catherine leaned over to grab a liter of bottled water. "You've had too much on you the last few months. Just make today a vacation day. Go shopping or something. Take Buddy for a walk. Forget about those sessions."

"It's not just that," I said. "With all this talk going around, Jill is giving me hell. She's more and more antagonistic every time I talk to her. And as usual, she's been working Luanne like a puppet. I think she really believes Jud and I are having an affair. She thinks I've turned into a lunatic who's intent on stirring up trouble just to make her life miserable."

After chugging down a long drink, Catherine said, "Willi, I'm not going to lie to you. You're right, she is extremely hot. She told me you were being flippant—her word—and careless about letting your personal life interfere with work."

"What personal life? I'm not seeing anyone, especially Jud. Don't tell me you think that too?"

"No, of course not." She took another swig and sighed heavily. "But something else is bothering her. All of us, really." She hesitated a moment trying to find the right words. "She is extremely pissed because of your behavior at Jud's studio."

"That's hardly worth mentioning. So we had a fight right after the session."

"Not then. The other time. At Jennalyn's party."

"Oh. Well, I can't help that. Jill's mad because she didn't believe I had been shot at the day before, and then we saw all those rifles in Jud's office right over the garden. She was wrong but won't admit it. It's her problem."

"That's not it, either," Catherine said before giving me the real kicker. "She and Luanne said you were falling-down drunk at the party. That you had to have help just to get out of the building. That you didn't only embarrass yourself, you embarrassed the two of them in front of a lot of important people."

Catherine rolled her chair closer to mine and took my hands in hers. "Willi, hon, listen to me. I understand. I have a friend who was in a similar situation. He had family problems, then he started drinking a little too much. It kind of sneaked up on him, and before he knew what was happening, things went from bad to worse."

I shook my head vigorously as I tightened my grip on her hands. "Who was it?" I asked, feeling a constriction in my chest. "Who did they see me with that night? Did they say?"

"I don't remember that they mentioned anyone specifically."

I stood up. "Thanks, Cath. I've gotta go. Don't worry about me, you hear?" I lightly slapped her on the arms.

"Will, don't be stubborn about asking for help . . . ."

I pursed my lips and gave her a mean look.

"*If* . . . I'm saying *if* you need it," she said.

"I don't have time to explain everything," I said. "For now, just take my word for it, okay? I am not a drunk."

"Good. When I talk to Jill, I'll give her that message."

I opened the door to let Buddy walk on out. "Not necessary," I said. "I'll tell her myself."

As I drove to Jud's complex on the river, I was red-hot and getting hotter. My temperature had been going up all morning anyway. That talk with Catherine was like striking a match next to dry kindling.

I've had sessions canceled before. It wasn't that. Usually they are rescheduled later and it's no big deal. Unless I'm really counting on the money right then.

But this was personal. To my knowledge, this was the first time I had been canceled when the sessions went on as planned.

Twice I turned around to go back home. Jill was right about one thing—I was changing. My old nature to run away and hide until the flack stops flying was giving way to a more aggressive person inside. The old me wanted to go home and crawl under the blankets. The emerging one knew I had to grow some balls and get on the offensive.

I needed this to be over. I wanted the comfort of my dull, normal life again. I kept telling myself Jill or Luanne must have seen someone suspicious around me at the party. If I got a name from them, I'd pass it on to Bracken. Then I could relax.

But first I had to reinvent myself for the next hour or so in order to confront both Jill and Jud. The thought of it scared me spitless and at the same time made me madder than hellfire. I wiped the sweat pouring off my forehead into my eyes and thought it would be a miracle if I made it to the complex before spontaneously combusting.

After winding around through the wooded acres on Jud's property, I parked out front near the studio door. I didn't go straight in. Sitting in the car, I closed my eyes and tried to breathe slowly while gathering my thoughts.

I would state my case calmly to Jill. She'd see how she'd misunderstood. When Jud saw that I'd heard his little lie and wasn't about to take it lying down, he'd back off and that would be the end of it. They'd both apologize and go away whimpering. Everything would be fine.

The lobby was empty. I fast-walked to the end of the photo gallery and turned toward Studio A.

Jill was standing behind Possum. He sat at the board trying to look like he knew what he was doing.

His eyes were closed and his stringy hair swung behind his neck. He was putting on a show, enjoying being the only guy in a roomful of women. I figured this was as close as he ever got to having sex, as ugly as he was.

With exaggerated effort, Possum dragged the master fader down slowly, making the end of the song fade out until the speakers were completely silent. All eyes were on him and he loved it. He brought his right hand up high, obviously pleased with himself.

I remained quiet while the three girls chatted in front of me—Jill, Luanne, and Amy Metke, a tall California blonde we'd done sessions with a few times before. She was a beautiful girl and very professional. I knew Jill probably considered getting Amy at the last minute a real coup. After this—six hours of master scale—Amy might feel a bit of an obligation to the girls and include them on some of her future sessions.

Possum stopped the tape machine and moved his arms back suddenly, probably hoping to accidentally cop a feel from one of the girls standing behind his chair. When they all took a step back, I stepped forward and cleared my throat.

Jill stared at me in disbelief. She came toward me with her hands on her hips and spoke in a low but cutting tone. "Did you misunderstand Luanne's message?"

I shrugged. "I don't think so."

"Then you might oughta leave, don't you reckon?"

I nodded. "Yeah. One quick question. At Jennalyn's party, did you see who was with me in the parking lot?"

Her head jerked back a few inches, not expecting this topic. She blinked a few times then said, "No. Why?" Luanne came over to us and also shook her head.

"What about anyone walking me out?"

Jill's eyebrows furrowed as she moved her long straight hair to fall down her back. "Can't you even remember who was around you? What does that tell you, Willi?"

"You told Catherine I had to be helped out the door. Did you or did you not see anyone with me that night? Just answer me and I'll get out of your superior hair."

Although I looked expectantly back and forth from Luanne to Jill, they couldn't seem to come up with anything definite. Apparently somebody told somebody else that somebody saw me with somebody.

A flicker on the producer's desk caught my eye. I walked over to the end of the console and looked down at the four TV screens beneath the glass top. Three of the four showed no activity. The last one, however, showed the top of two men's heads.

Pointing to them, I asked Possum if he knew where that particular camera was. He hitched his thumb toward the door. "The big hall," he said. Without saying good-bye, I walked out with a chip on my shoulder and no idea what I would say to Jud.

My heart pounded in my head as I knocked the two air-lock doors out of my way and raced back toward the main hallway. Although I knew I should be walking slowly in order to gather my thoughts, I couldn't help it, fearing I would talk myself out of confronting Jud if I didn't hurry.

Just as I rounded the corner at the end of the hall, Jud and Tom, the producer who fired me from the day's sessions, looked up. Their conversation stopped as soon as they saw me. Each gave me a dismissive look which, in my younger days, would have been enough to send me running and crying. That day, it only made me madder.

I took a step closer to Jud and did not blink as I let the fire burn higher in my eyes. Whatever cutesy remark he had in mind fizzled away as I stood my ground. I let my purse drop with a loud thud and said, "Jud," in as calm a tone as I could muster.

Tom patted Jud lightly on the back. "I'm gonna run on and let you talk to your lady friend. Catch up with you later, son." He gave him a knowing wink which Jud returned.

I found myself studying Jud's thick neck, the width of his midsection. I realized I had unconsciously wrapped my purse strap around the knuckles of my right hand.

"What are you doing to me?" I spoke softly, gently pulling my purse up and down as if testing its weight. When I stepped closer, Jud moved backward.

"I'm sorry?" he said with a high-and-mighty smile.

"WHAT . . . ," I yelled while suddenly throwing my purse into his stomach, ". . . are you DOING . . . ," punching him again in the ribs, ". . . to ME?"

It was the third jab, one that would have slammed up into his chin if he hadn't jerked away, that woke me up. Jud wasn't even half as shocked as I was at myself. Breathing hard, I could feel spit at the corners of my mouth. I'd never hit anyone before, outside of just horsing around, not with the intention of doing real damage.

Yanking the purse back by the strap, I could feel my fingers throbbing as I threw it back on the floor. For a moment I felt a little release and thought, *maybe that was enough.* Maybe now, with that out my system, I could get hold of myself. *Two adults and all that,* I thought, until I saw his reaction.

He laughed. It was only a wheeze at first, way down in his throat. But soon, his belly was jiggling and his hands held his sides. He pointed upward and said, "I hope I got that on tape!"

"Look at me! You tell me why you're spreading lies about me!"

"Willi, Willi," he said, still chuckling. "I don't know what you're talking about. You're an excitable little thing, I tell you the truth! What's got you so riled up? Or is it just that time of the month, sweetheart?"

Planting my left leg out in front of me, I swung the purse behind me and let it fly again. He was ready for me this time and successfully blocked the serve.

"Tell me!" I yelled. "What did I ever do to you?"

"Now, Willi, you quit it and settle down, you hear? You didn't used to be like this. Why, look up there at yourself," he said, indicating the blown-up photograph near us of Jennalyn's first session. "You were the sweetest little child I believe I've ever seen. And look at you now. It's your choice, babe, but you might want to reevaluate yourself. I don't know what happened to you."

"Are you going after me out of sport? Was it not enough to try to pick me off with your rifle—now you're trying to shoot down my career?" I paused again, expecting another blanket denial. "That's it, isn't it? A power trip. Because you can. You're like a hunter that kills just because he can do it and get away with it. Because it amuses him to watch something innocent bleed and die in the woods, isn't that it, Jud?"

Some dark thought moved across Jud's eyes. His facial muscles clamped and twitched beneath his skin. His face grew redder as his breathing came out in short huffs.

"You're out of your mind," he finally said. "I think you need to go home and get some rest. Either that or go see a doctor."

*This is hopeless*, I thought. I glanced once more at the old photo of us and Jennalyn.

"You spineless bastard," I said, clenching my jaws almost

completely shut. "You let me hear that you've said one more word about me, and the next professional I see won't be a doctor—it'll be a lawyer. One more word, and I swear I'll bear down on you where it really hurts—your wallet and your freakin' career."

A jolt went through him, beginning at his scalp and wiggling out the tips of his fingers. He recovered quickly, but I knew I'd hit a nerve. "Get out of here," he said, his voice low and strained.

I smacked my palm hard, flat against the glass-covered photograph. Whether I struck out at Jud's younger self or my own, I couldn't say. I smacked it again, right at Jennalyn's neck, leaning all my weight into my hand. It's a wonder I didn't shatter the frame and cut my hands to ribbons. As angry as I was, I probably wouldn't have felt a thing.

"Get off my property!" he said.

"You get off my back!" I pushed away from the wall and stormed past him.

"And stay off! You'll never work here again!" I heard Jud say behind me. When I reached the lobby I spun around, planning to fling a parting insult.

But the hall was empty. Jud had vanished without a sound.

I drove back to Sam's office. Since I needed to work off some energy, I snapped Buddy's leash on and the two of us headed out for a brisk walk.

The sidewalk was blazing hot and the air so thick with car exhaust, I almost changed my mind. But Buddy seemed happy to be out and doing something. I felt too guilty to let him down.

It wasn't far to the grassy stretch on the other side of Alabama Avenue, a road that runs behind Charlotte. After Buddy did his business, we continued toward the intersection at 46th Avenue, where I saw a familiar figure at the walk signal button waiting to cross.

Macie was a sight. She wore a mint green polyester pantsuit over a multi-colored floral shirt. I couldn't believe she was wearing a jacket, even a lightweight one, in the heat. The slacks were high-waters, hemmed two or three inches above her ankles. At least she had on tennis shoes, and I wondered how she managed to make her usual rounds on such a hot day with no hat. Her only protection from the sun was a flimsy green clip-on shade that was too big over her cat-eye glasses.

We caught up with her in the middle of the crosswalk as the yellow caution light came on. For a while, Buddy and I walked beside her without talking. She was in the middle of a conversation with herself and I hated to interrupt.

As best I could tell, the topic of the day involved the FBI; Macie's second cousin Mildred, who ran a fabric store in Paducah; and Mildred's psychic daughter, Glenda, a part-time nurse who foresaw the assassination of JFK.

"Where you headed, Macie?" I asked as we stepped into the shade of the interstate bridge above us. I was glad of a little cooler air not just for my sake, but for Macie who didn't look well to me.

"Home, I reckon," she said weakly. She looked around her, front and back, as if she wasn't sure where she was. "Yeah. Home."

Coming out of the shade, we waited for a light change to cross again. Sitting on the corner in front of us gleamed the glass and chrome of Hawg Wild Motorcycles.

"You mind if Buddy and I walk with you?"

"It's not far," she said. Her steps were uneven. Several times I thought she would've toppled over if I hadn't put my hand on her back for balance. She felt so fragile, as if she would crumble and blow away in a gust of wind. At first, I considered her wobbling might be a ploy. I hadn't forgotten how she picked my pocket. This time it was no act. Her words became softer as her mind wandered through other obsessions, touching here and there on scraps of memories and stringing them together.

Hawg Wild was the only business on its block. All around it were small wood-frame houses, the official beginning of the Nations, an older low-income neighborhood. I felt an unexpected surge of fear as we passed the motorcycle shop. I supposed it was due to Horace and Dorace. The twins were formidably built, so their size alone was enough to make me uncomfortable. Their permanent scowls and minimalist, slow way of talking only worsened matters, making them top candidates for my "Mean Rednecks To Avoid" list.

We walked left across the front of the building toward a two-story elementary school on the next block.

"Down this way," Macie said as she motioned with her handbag and cut the corner of the cycle shop's front parking lot. Trees lined the street that ran between the shop and the school's playground, giving us another welcome break of cooler air.

The playground lot wasn't so lucky. With little grass and no trees, it looked dusty and desolate with the dull glint of the sun cooking the metal slides and swing bars. *No wonder the park is empty*, I thought. *The kids were no fools.*

The sound of revving engines jerked our attention to the rear service entrance of the cycle shop. Several bikers yelled over the motors' noise to each other. I recognized two of the hulking figures as the Wilcox brothers. Their friends weren't runts, either. Even from that distance, I could make out the blues and reds of elaborate tattoos covering their extra-large biceps and disappearing into their tank tops.

Dorace had worn an orange work coverall the time I'd seen him, so I figured he was the one getting up off his knee and brushing it off. He'd been inspecting one of the revving bikes and, on standing, happened to see me and Macie watching them.

Both of us turned away abruptly and walked a little faster. The unfamiliar neighborhood was starting to give me the creeps. The deserted school, black behind its windows, reminded me of an abandoned factory. Nothing moved inside it; still I felt as if eyes were on us. Macie reached up to her throat, running her hand along the bones of her neck when something clicked in my mind. I couldn't grasp it in time, and it was gone.

"They don't know what they're doing," Macie said softly.

"Who, those bikers?"

"No," she said. "The FBI. If they did, Glenda would be right up there working with them, psyching things out for the government. She wouldn't have to be working two part-time jobs and selling BeautyWares. She could just use her mind."

Another loud burst of noise made me jump. It sounded louder and closer than before. While I hoped the bikers hadn't seen that they'd scared me, I saw Buddy jump, too, and flatten his stomach to the ground.

Before his odd reaction could register, I felt a wet spray on my face and arm. Out of the corner of my eye, I saw Macie moving, slipping down.

When I reached out to her, my arm looked unfamiliar, a foreign object splotched from end to end in red. Although perhaps only a second, two seconds had passed, it seemed an eternity as I watched everything suddenly move in slow motion.

I caught her before she hit the ground, sliding my free arm under her back and dropping Buddy's leash. Macie's body felt like a sparrow, hardly big or heavy enough to contain a life. On her right side, the one closest to me, a red stain spread quickly over the jacket. The skinny arm dangling beside her was the source. I pushed up the sleeve to find blood spurting from the bend of the elbow. The meat of her thin arm had been ripped away, exposing the bone.

It wasn't until another loud blast rang out over us that I knew what was happening. Macie had been shot. And whoever had done it wasn't finished.

I couldn't see her eyes, just the thin lines of blood spattered across the clip-on shades. She was conscious but dazed. The second shot made her start screaming and groping with her other arm. I rolled to the opposite side, scooping her up and lurching forward in a low crouch. I scooted us behind an old Buick parked on the road. Two more rounds fired, one pinging off a tree trunk, the other off the Buick's fender.

Macie's shrieks became moans as she writhed in pain. I huddled over her, taking the shades off her glasses. With her head in my hands, I made her look at me while I said, "Everything's all right. Everything's going to be fine," over and over again.

A wet nose nuzzled my face. I hugged Buddy to me and could feel him shaking as I pressed him down close to Macie. "Good boy. Stay. Stay right here." He whimpered his consent and began licking Macie's face as her weak fingers found refuge in his coat.

Looking around us, I thought we were fairly safe until I heard the rumble of motorcycles coming closer. A bike would have no trouble jumping the curb and riding circles around us. We'd be sitting ducks. Why were they after me?

Under the Buick, a rusty muffler lay on the asphalt. Seeing no other weapon for our defense, I grabbed it. Raising myself on the balls of my feet, I crept toward the trunk and peeped from behind the taillight. Coming toward me was a motorcycle driven by a big man in an orange coverall, the handlebars in one huge hand, a long-barreled handgun in the other. I ducked and heard two deafening shots, the sound of rubber squealing on the pavement, and an explosive crash of glass and metal.

Bits of shattered glass pelted the old Buick that shielded us. The crash was so close, I thought it might be Dorace's motorcycle, but I could hear it still, rumbling closer. Tires crunched over glass, then a *whump-ump* as the bike jumped the curb.

I was ready to spring when the front wheel came into view. Gripping the muffler, I stood up and took a swipe at Dorace's arm in hopes of knocking his gun away.

I missed. Dorace glanced quickly down at Macie, then at me, as he whooshed by. "Hey!" he yelled, passing and taking another look at us in his rearview mirror. He turned his bike around in the school yard to come toward me again. I shouldered the muffler like a bat and prepared to try again.

"Stop that!" Dorace yelled. "I'm trying to help you!" Making a tight circle, he passed once more and said, "Stay down!" before goosing the handlebar and riding away.

I walked to the other end of the Buick. Peeping out at

headlight level, I saw what had crashed. A Honda Accord had smashed against a light pole at the edge of the playground. Dorace was cutting a wide arc around it. He held his gun out toward it as he drove, looking like a jouster ready to spar.

"Come outta that car!" he yelled to the figure at the wheel.

I crept around the Buick's hood and looked to the left. The three other bikes we'd seen earlier idled side by side, blocking the road. Each man held a gun.

Now I could see the reason for the crash—a back tire was flat. From the looks on the bikers' faces as they caressed their guns, it wasn't much of a leap to guess what caused it. Horace Wilcox, wearing plain denim overalls, rumbled forward from the line and stopped opposite his brother, who had taken a position behind the Honda.

Suddenly the car lurched into reverse. It smoked and squealed as rubber burned in an attempt to escape. Shots flamed out the window at Dorace. The Honda moved less than ten feet farther into the playground before a barrage of gunfire expertly shot out the remaining three tires.

"It's over—throw out your weapon!" Horace said.

Dust spewed and settled into the ruts ground out by the car's wheel rims. Giving up, the driver of the Honda cut off his engine. About ten seconds passed before a pistol was tossed out into the dirt.

"Now come out—real slow." Horace leaned onto one leg and put down the kickstand, never taking his eyes off the car or lowering his gun.

With the Honda now angled backwards, its front faced me and I could see its dented grill. This was the car that had followed me from Jud's studio right after someone shot at me.

As the car door creaked open, I moved onto the playground. Going toward the car, I walked between a slide and a carousel with low railings. I wanted to get a good look at the person who wanted me dead.

Putting his hands out first, Martin Schaefer Jr. slowly got out of his wrecked car. He had on an expensive-looking jacket and tie, as if he'd just come from his law office or from court.

"Don't shoot!" he said. His halting steps looked as shaky as his voice sounded. Looking furtively from one biker to another, he stepped away from each in turn, finally backing away in my direction. "Please," he stuttered, "Don't . . . don't shoot."

On the other side of the Honda, Dorace Wilcox pressed a button on the console of his bike and brought the receiver of a cellular phone to his ear.

"We've got a situation here," he said. "We need the police and an ambulance pronto." Dorace alternately wiped his hands on the legs of his orange coverall while he gave the 911 operator our location.

"Why?" I yelled. Martin Jr. still looked from man to man. He kept his back turned to me and pretended not to hear. This so infuriated me that I strode up to his back, grabbed his arm, and spun him around.

"Why?" I asked again, but this time I screamed it in his face. "Answer me! You think I won't beat you senseless? You think these guys are the type to want to stop me?"

Two large stains of sweat spread on his jacket under his armpits. He wiped his eyes dry with one hand while still holding the other up. Taking one more glance at Horace, the nearest man to us, he shook his head and leaned toward me.

"No," he said. "But I do think—" Suddenly he yanked my arms and pressed my back into his body. He clamped his left arm over my chest, pinning me to him. I was a good shield. I could see Horace and Dorace both grip their weapons and almost fire before stopping themselves. At the same time, Martin reached into his jacket. My neck froze as I felt the cold end of a gun barrel nudge into my cheekbone.

"—I *do* think," he continued, breathing hard, "they're the type to give me a motorcycle." Martin eyed the one nearest, Horace's bike.

Horace snorted a short laugh. "I can't see that happening, bud," he said. Although he smiled, he clearly did not intend to push his bluff.

"You're going to let me take it or I'll blow her head off."

He squeezed me tighter until I thought he'd break my ribs. His words were strained, but they had a cold edge of control. He was used to thinking on his feet and improvising in order to win in court. This time, his life depended on it.

As Horace stepped slowly away from his motorcycle, Martin said, "That's better." He dragged me along with him, careful to keep me between him and the others. "Don't follow and don't shoot," he said. "If you do, I kill her and throw her in the street."

"Like you're not planning on it anyway," I mumbled.

His breath was hot on my neck. His lips touched my earlobe as he said, "Oh, I don't know . . . we might go somewhere and have a little fun first." His arm locked tighter while he pressed me against his crotch. "You're useful," he whispered. "For now."

With a backward jerk, he pulled me to the bike. When I made no attempt to climb on, he jabbed the gun further into my cheek.

"Swing your leg over!" he said. "Do it now!"

My mind raced, picturing the scenario of us riding away, of him shooting me and dumping me, probably not far from here to make a quick getaway. He'd be caught eventually, I knew that. But it was small comfort since I'd be a goner by then.

"Okay, okay," I said and shifted my weight to the left. I brought my right knee up slowly. In the distance, a police siren made Martin flinch.

I kicked my leg back as hard as I could, down into his shin. The gun slipped to my neck as Martin's grip loosened around my chest. Although he still held me, I was able to move my arms up as I kicked. I grabbed his wrist and wrapped my foot behind his ankle and pushed with all my might, praying his finger wasn't on the trigger.

As I threw my full weight into him, we staggered a few steps backward and smacked into the children's slide. His shoulders hit about midway as I turned out of his grip and bent his gun arm over the rim. I pressed it hard with both hands until his wrist and knuckles were flat against the burning hot metal.

He screamed in pain and relaxed his fingers slightly, enough to send the gun clattering down the slide to rest at the bottom edge. With a grunt, he pushed my arms away and both of us dived for the gun.

I let go a series of wild kicks, not caring where they landed. This bought me a few seconds, long enough to get a tenuous grip on the gun and pitch it away as far as I could. It flew a few feet and rattled to a stop on the wooden boards of the playground carousel.

Both Martin and I crawled on all fours toward it. He beat me to it and, still on his knees, stretched out for the gun between the curved iron rails. All I could do was throw myself onto the carousel. Just before his fingers touched the gun's handle, the little merry-go-round spun clockwise, carrying the weapon out of his reach.

"You bitch!" he yelled. "Sam was easy compared to you."

In that instant the whirling carousel became the blur of newspaper microfiche, and the murdered teenager's picture clicked into place by the photo of Jennalyn like two pieces of a jigsaw puzzle.

Grief and fury swelled up in me. I clenched my teeth and rammed the iron railing forward again, catching Martin across the temple. The blow knocked his head out from between the bars. His body followed and fell limp in the dirt. With a vicious kick to his collarbone, I rolled him over on his back.

Straddling his belly, I dropped to my knees and sat on his chest. I was about to hit him when the scent of his cologne caught me, reminding me of the night I'd been drugged. He was the one who had taken me to the cemetery. The one who'd beaten me up.

My left hand felt like a bear claw, heavy and lethal, as I pushed his head down hard into the dirt. With a low growl, I cocked my right arm behind me, ready to punch.

Before I could swing, huge arms lifted me up and off of Martin. Horace Wilcox held me, swinging and cussing, while the two tattooed bikers dragged Martin in the other direction.

Beyond them, I could see the blue flashing lights of police cars. Seeing several officers advancing toward us, I stopped fighting Horace. When a policeman passed the old Buick, Buddy jumped up and started barking to get his attention. The patrolman ran back to Macie, knelt over her, and called the medic.

My breathing was ragged, gasping in and sobbing out. As Horace set me gently to my feet, the little wooden carousel brought Martin's gun around its circle, creaking to a stop in front of me.

A few minutes later, a motorcycle rumbled up and parked behind us. Dorace Wilcox dismounted and ambled over next to his brother. When he got closer, I could see Dorace was sniffling. He kept rubbing his face, then ran his hands up over his eyes in a manly attempt to cover up the fact that he was crying.

I was touched. I felt bad for misjudging him earlier, thinking him nothing more than a dumb redneck. Not only had he cared enough to rescue us, he now showed real sympathy as he looked off toward Macie and the ambulance.

"You all right, bud?" Horace said to him.

Dorace pursed his lips into a thin line. He wiped his hands on the legs of his orange coverall and paused a moment, trying to contain his emotion before speaking in a very soft voice.

"He dinged my hog," he said quietly.

Horace and I looked at Dorace's bike and the two bullet holes that pierced its otherwise immaculate finish.

"He *dinged* my *hog*, man!" Dorace said in a girlish voice as he wept into his shirt sleeve. His shoulders shook as he fell to his knees and caressed the defiled metal work, grieving at the sin against art that was, to him, right up there with the desecration of the Pietà.

# CHAPTER 14

"NOT MUCH LONGER," Detective Bracken said. He ushered me into his cubicle and pulled a chair out for me. "I know you're tired of talking. Hang with me. I'll turn you loose as soon as I can."

After Macie had been taken away in the ambulance, I'd left the Wilcox brothers and the other bikers still giving their accounts. I found out Horace and Dorace had been my guardian angels. Since Sam's death, they'd kept an eye on me after Uncle Ralph told them about my break-in.

I'd already given my statement to a patrolman on the scene and asked him to call Bracken for me; I had a lot to run by him.

Bracken looked over the report on his desk for a few minutes. "Glad you're okay," he said. "Lucky for you, Schaefer is a lousy shot."

"*And*," I said, "that the cavalry was close enough to rescue me."

The bikers had seen the black Honda follow me and Macie, then make a sudden turn to circle the block. When the car came down an alley and appeared to wait for us, Dorace knew something was wrong. He had already jumped on his bike when Martin shot and Macie went down. While reaching into his saddlebag for his gun, he cut straight across the shop's backyard as Martin fired again.

Bracken nodded as he read down the report. "They should have frisked him," he said.

"It all happened so fast," I said. "It was my fault. I walked right up to him. The last thing I expected was for him to have two guns."

He stared at me. "So, this is your guy, the one who's been

giving you grief?"

"Yeah. What has Martin had to say for himself?"

Bracken smiled. "It was an accident."

"What?" I said in disbelief.

"He says he was driving by when the gun went off accidentally. That when he saw Dorace shooting at him, he got scared and lost it. It's a weak story and he knows it."

"Can't you do a good cop/bad cop routine on him and make him talk?"

From the other side of Bracken's cubicle, I heard a couple of the other detectives laugh. "Yeah! Go sit on him, big boy!" one of them said.

"I'll do it," Bracken said. "Then you or Yates can kiss him and make him all better."

The laughter died down and Bracken said to me, "That sort of thing might work on ordinary scum, but not too well on a lawyer. But don't worry. According to Dorace, Martin shot Macie, then fired into the parked Buick before Dorace fired at him. I expect ballistics to blow the accident story apart."

"Good," I said. "Either way, though, he's going to confess."

"Oh? Why's that?"

"Because you're going to make him a deal. I guarantee, his buddies in all this are going to leave him high and dry. When he realizes that, he'll roll over like a dead guppy. Then you, my friend, will be the next chief of police."

"Hah! I'm flattered you have such confidence in me. Do you have a crystal ball, or is any of this based on fact?"

"A little of both at this point," I said and paused, not for a dramatic effect but because I didn't know where to start.

"You think Schaefer killed Sam," Bracken prodded.

"Yes." I told him what Martin said when we were struggling for his gun on the playground.

"He'll deny it. And I can tell you right now, neither of those guns of his will match up to Sam's murder weapon."

"If he had two guns, he could easily have had a third one and thrown it away," I said. "Anyway, it doesn't matter. With him in the picture, it all makes sense now."

"You said 'his buddies.'"

I nodded. "I think Sam had some incriminating information on them, so serious that Martin killed him.

"The night he died, I had an unusually long session with Rick Crawford—he's one. His job was to keep me busy while Martin was at Sam's office, looking for any written record of him or the others. Whether Sam was expecting him or caught him breaking in, I don't know.

"When nothing turned up in his search, Martin took my apartment key off Sam's ring and searched my place the same night. His wife is an old friend of mine, so he knew my full name. My address is in the phone book.

"A few days after my break-in, someone takes a potshot at me at Jud's studio. I'm not sure if it was Jud or his son Blaine. He's the second partner. Then a black Honda with a dented grill follows me home. Martin's car.

"They must have been unsure how much I knew about Sam's business, and decided to keep an eye on me rather than risk another murder. I saw the same car earlier that day," I said, remembering when Macie stole my pack of gum on the sidewalk. The Honda sat facing us from Richland Park, right across from Sam's office.

"Rick. Blaine. Martin. Ring any bells?" I asked, reaching for my coffee cup.

"The three Sam busted for possession in 1978," Bracken said. He turned his hands up in the air in a *so what?* gesture.

"Wait. They get worried when they see me talking to you. Martin catches me spying on his sister's house. Now it looks like I'm continuing Sam's case against them. That's when they decide to turn up the heat. They drug me and try to scare me off at Jennalyn's party. I didn't see Martin, but Rick and Blaine were both there."

"Ms. Taft, all this is speculation," Bracken said. "The bust was a long time ago and everybody knew about it. I mean, what would be the point? Why would they be worried twenty years after the fact? Did Sam suspect them of selling drugs now?"

"No," I said. "He suspected them of murder." I pulled my

purse up into my lap and took out the two enlargements from Waldo's. "The drug bust was the night of Jennalyn's first session. It was also two days before Casey Lanham was found dead in the park. I think they killed her and Sam was on to them."

Bracken looked stunned. "We found nothing that would suggest that in Sam's files," he said. "Unless you've found something new."

"Just these," I said and explained how I'd picked up the pictures.

Bracken squinted at the photos of Paris. I reached across the desk and pointed out Stephanie and Casey. "Dressed identically," he said. "They look like sisters."

"Yeah. The same clothes down to their necklaces. Can you see them? Each has fifteen beads—one for each birthday. It's the kind girls used to buy where you add a new bead on each year. I don't know why I didn't make the connection before now. Look at this close-up. The girls had them specially engraved. Stephanie's has the word *Friends* on hers, Casey's says *Forever*.

"Hey, Ronnie," Bracken yelled. "Bring me the file on Casey Lanham—scene photos and the list of her effects." He studied the picture a moment and said, "It's been a long time, but I don't recall this in evidence."

I shook my head while I swallowed a hot sip of coffee. "It won't be there."

"You sound pretty sure of yourself."

I shrugged. "I know where it is. And how it got there."

Thirty minutes later, I drove to St. Thomas Hospital to pick up Macie. Since her sister's shift at the boot factory wouldn't end for a few hours, I had assured her on the phone I'd be glad to take her home.

Bracken had listened attentively to my theory about Casey Lanham's death. I wasn't sure I'd convinced him, but I knew I was right. The good-luck necklace given to Jennalyn by Blaine had to be Casey's.

As I turned into the hospital parking lot, I tried to put it all aside for the moment. The police would be the ones to examine the photos and the necklaces, not me. It was officially out of my hands and it would do me no good to worry.

It was time to forget the past and concentrate on the present. I had only one task for now—to see Macie safely home.

After winding through the halls in St. Thomas's emergency ward, I entered the room where Macie rested. I should say, the room where she was supposed to be resting. When I opened the door, she was rolling across the floor on the doctor's stool. Her arm was bent in a sling, but otherwise she looked fine. She had propped her compact open on the end of the examination table. With her right hand, she flicked the cap off a lipstick tube and drew thick red lines around her mouth.

"Hey, you're looking good," I said. "You about ready to go home?"

Macie pushed her heels into the floor, scooting the stool back to the sink cabinet. She took a tissue from a box, folded it, and pressed her lips together over it.

"I reckon," she said, snapping a few extras out and stuffing them into her purse. Her eyes widened on opening a drawer full of shiny medical instruments. Before she could make a selection, I gently guided her up and out the door.

On the way to her house, I wished I had known her address beforehand. I'd have gone the long way around to avoid passing where she had been shot. But as it was, I had to follow her directions. When we turned past the motorcycle shop, it didn't seem to bother her at all to see the scene of the crime.

"Them policemen was right there, wasn't they?" she said as we drove by the playground.

"They sure were," I said.

"Turn right here," Macie said, patting the dashboard. "Mine is the yellow house."

Paint peeled on the wooden siding and trim work of the little one-story cottage. There was no driveway. I pulled behind a station wagon parked on the street out in front.

"There's Sandra," Macie said, undoing her seat belt.

The woman coming out the front door covered her look

of anguish with her hands when she saw Macie's arm bandaged and trussed. Like her sister, Sandra was tall and thin. The buttons of her cotton shirt, a plaid of pinks and greens, bulged a little across the chest. Her brownish-gray hair was pinned up and back under a hair net.

She acknowledged me with a nod and took charge, running her hands down Macie's hair as if she were comforting a child. Macie raised her good arm to bat Sandra away. The two of them chattered at the same time as they went up the cracked sidewalk.

"Stop that!" Macie said. "I don't want you a-worrying over me."

"What am I gonna do with you?" Sandra asked.

". . . always treat me like I hadn't got good sense . . . ."

"Well, you don't act like it half the time."

Pulling the screen closed after me, I stepped behind them into Macie's living room. A slight musty smell hung in the air with a strong overlay of rose potpourri and cigarette smoke. The sofa and chairs had green chenille slipcovers with fringe that brushed the hardwood floor.

"Let me get her settled into bed. Then we can talk," Sandra said as she led Macie toward a back hallway.

"I ain't going to bed—it's too early." Macie pulled away from her sister. She set her purse on the sofa and toddled over to a small end table draped in a crocheted cloth. On it, an odd assortment of trinkets and pictures was spread around the bases of three pillar candles and several votives. Above it on the wall hung a rendition of the Virgin Mary. Beside it was an antique hand-painted lithograph. Its caption, ON GUARD, was below the picture of a dog watching over a child asleep in a meadow.

Macie opened the table's single drawer. "I'm not a-goin' to bed. I'm gonna light my candles. All this meanness wouldn't never have happened if I'd a-been lighting my candles regular."

She fumbled with a box of matches as she talked. She was able to slide it open but, having to use her left hand, had a hard time getting a match out. Frustrated, she began mumbling and crying and becoming more agitated.

"Here, let me do that for you." Her hand shook as I took the box from her. Striking a match on the side, I asked, "Which ones?"

"All of 'em. I need all of 'em." With two big tears running down her cheeks, she swayed nervously from left to right, then pushed her sister toward the windows and said, "Close the drapes, close the drapes!"

Sandra complied. Going over to the side window she reached high to yank the heavy curtains together, then did the front ones that hung behind an old-fashioned milk-glass lamp. The curtains were dark, a maroon that made the afternoon light turn the room different shades of red and rose.

Sandra came up behind Macie and hugged her close. "Now you come on," she said, talking softly. "Let's get you out of these clothes." Macie allowed herself to be taken away with the promise of cigarettes and a bubble bath. The old floorboards creaked down the hall as the sisters left me alone to my task at the altar.

As the match touched each wick, it lit a small world of mementos—buttons, loose settings of rhinestones, an old watch with no band or crystal, a few sea shells. Among them, family pictures and school photos of children were arranged around the candles.

In the tall glass holders, flames glowed behind the faces of saints on prayer candles. I picked up one with the picture of a woman holding a gold chalice and a sword. The novena on its side said OH LORD, KEEP AWAY THE WICKED, MISERABLE PEOPLE WHO LURK IN THE SHADOWS SEEKING TO HARM ME.

The light from the last two votives brought a sight I couldn't believe. I stood bent over, looking at a snapshot of Sam with his head thrown back laughing. His arm was around Macie in front of the pawn shop. On the table beside it, leaning against an old blue powder box made of tin, was a cassette tape. Its label made my heart clutch as it glowed in the fuzz of candlelight: JULY 20TH—the day of Sam's murder, written in his own handwriting.

Macie and Sandra bantered softly behind the walls.

Somewhere in the back of the house, a window air conditioner roared to life. The following whoosh moved what sounded like tiny wind chimes, the cheap kind you win at the fair, in its breeze.

I don't know how long I stared at the tape, considering its contents, picturing Sam's hand scribble across it, hearing his laugh come out of the picture and float among the chimes and flickering lights. Sam wouldn't have given it to Macie, she must have taken it from his pocket.

The floor creaked in the hallway as Sandra's steps came closer. With only a moment's hesitation, I stuck the cassette in my pocket, promising myself to replace it soon with something pretty.

The only bad thing about the Malibu was it didn't have a cassette player. Since I couldn't listen to Sam's tape on the way to the office, I turned the radio to the progressive station in town.

An interview was in progress. When I heard the DJ mention the featured band's name, I turned up the volume. The station had been playing a few of their songs recently that I thought were good.

The band had relocated to Nashville but still had their west-coast accents. After a few run-of-the-mill questions, the DJ asked, "So, guys, how do you like living here? You already have a record deal with a major label, a nationwide tour coming up . . . ."

"Right. Nashville's been good to us," one of the band members answered. "We all had doubts at first about moving so far . . . away—"

"Yeah," another one said, "but when we realized everyone here is from somewhere else too—the Midwest, New York, L.A.—it was so cool! It's like we're not even in the South."

"That's true," the first voice said. "The city has changed tremendously the last few years with people from all over the country moving in. Nashville's really a great place now that we're all here."

If I had been in my own car and not in a 1968 Malibu

Classic in mint condition, I'd have ripped the radio's buttons all off. Instead, I gave it one good pop to shut them up.

I had to slam on my brakes when a car cut in front of me. "Whaddya think this is, the New Jersey Turnpike?" I said as I looked around us at the uncrowded lanes.

I felt my anger from the radio interview focus on the car when I saw that it embodied several of my pet peeves. The driver was talking into his car phone; he drove a BMW; on his back window was a sticker from the campus down the road—Vanderbilt University, the southernmost Yankee outpost in the continental U.S. with the exception of the state of Florida.

I laid down on my horn and hollered, "You swarm of sorry locusts!" at the top of my lungs. For the next mile, I rode not more than a half-inch off his bumper until we stopped at a red light.

I was about to throw the gear shift into park so I could get out and tell him what I thought of him. But before I could, a little old lady eased her Taurus beside the BMW.

As much as I wanted to stay angry, I couldn't keep from laughing. Instead of numbers, her Tennessee car tag read BE SWEET, the admonition used most often by Southern mamas, grandmamas, aunts, and Sunday school teachers.

Watching its plume of black exhaust, I let the Beemer go.

# CHAPTER 15

THE ANSWERING MACHINE on Sam's desk blinked twice. While I rummaged through the packing boxes looking for his tape player, I listened to the messages.

The first one was from Jake. "You won't believe what I got today. It's too good to leave on the machine. Call me back as soon as possible."

An out-of-breath Douglas Anne Pennington left the second message. "Willi, you remember I told you somebody was breaking in my house? Well, I caught him! Yes, ma'am, I caught him red-handed, moving my figurines into dirty positions again! The police have just carted the worthless bum off to jail. Oh, he was the *ugliest* so-and-so. It was him that ran me off the road and messed up my Cadillac! I recognized his beat-up old car. I believe he's that hit-and-run fella, too, who put poor Stephanie in the hospital.

"And do you know what else? He was stealing my photo albums! He wouldn't say anything while he was here, but the police found a business card in his car. You'll never believe— it was Martin Schaefer's! I have to go, the police are knocking on my door again. I'll talk to you later."

Jake picked up on the first ring.

"You're not going to believe what I got today," he said after I greeted him.

"Whatever it is, it can't top my day. I was almost a corpse."

He listened patiently to my recount of events, asking a question here and there. When I finished he said, "That's it?"

"Isn't it enough? What, your news is more exciting?"

"You're not going to believe it," he said. "I got a letter."

I waited. "And?"

"And a confession tape from my dearly departed partner, Martin Schaefer. Seems he got a case of conscience before he kicked over. He left instructions with his estate lawyer to send me this packet. Here, listen to this."

In the phone, I heard Jake push a button. A tape whirred, then the gravelly voice of Martin Schaefer Sr. spoke from the grave:

"Jake, old son, you're probably surprised to hear from me after all these years. I guess I'm in the ground if you're hearing this. So many times I've wanted to call you, go get a beer like the old days. After hearing what I have to say, you'll understand why I couldn't risk it. It's too late to care anymore.

"Years ago I did something I thought I'd never do. I destroyed evidence in a murder case. I had to, Jake. My son, Marty, came to me for help. I had to do it.

"He told me his friend, Jud Sherrill's boy, had killed a girl. It was an accident, he told me. He said she was flirting with Blaine, and next thing he knew they were going at it in the back of a friend's van. Said she changed her mind when it was too late and went berserk. In the struggle she hit her head. When the boys realized she was dead, they panicked."

The tape clicked like it had been cut off. Seconds passed before it clicked again, and the dying man let out a long sigh before continuing:

"It was Casey Lanham, Jake. Right off, I told Marty they needed to go downtown. If it was an accident, they had nothing to worry about. He said, 'You didn't go downtown when Mom died.' I knew what he meant. It was blackmail. Lucy's death was ruled accidental. But the truth is, Jake . . . ."

Schaefer cleared his throat and paused. He took a deep breath and spoke as if the words hurt as he forced them out.

"The truth is, I did it. I hit her. We had an argument and I slapped her. I didn't mean to hit her so hard. Both kids were home. I made them lie. They told the doctor and Chief Perkins she fell. None of us ever mentioned it again.

"He told me where they put Casey. I went to the park in

— 180 —

a patrol car that night. Figured if anyone saw me, I'd call it in like I found her. From the first look, I knew they had lied. You saw the finger markings all around her neck.

"On the way home, I drove by Jud's studio. When I saw the boys in the parking lot being arrested for possession, I thought it was all over. Sam Robbins and I got into it when I tried to take over. I couldn't stop him from taking them in. It took some fancy footwork, but I managed to keep them from being booked and fingerprinted.

"Between me and Jud, we pulled enough strings to get them off. He assured me there'd be no problem in furnishing alibis if the boys needed them. He had loyal employees who would do what he asked with no questions.

"I sat up all night, smoking and drinking coffee. After racking my brain I finally figured out what I had to do. It was already daylight outside so I went on to work early.

"I found the most recent rape/murder case on file, wrote down the victim's name, and went down to the lab. The case was less than two days old, and I knew the guys down there were backed up. I'd seen where they kept the incoming cases. I pretended to have questions about a murder I'd been working. After the examiner's assistant went to take a phone call, I found the file I wanted easily and put it and the evidence bags in my briefcase.

"Then all I had to do was wait. When the call came in that Casey's body had been found, I went to the scene. After the team bagged all the samples, I volunteered to take everything to the lab. On the way, I stopped off at the house and switched everything with the samples I'd stolen.

"No new leads came in on Casey. Nobody had seen anything. I looked through the other girl's file a few weeks later. Tests on the semen and skin under her fingernails showed she was attacked by three men. I never told Marty I knew the truth about what he'd done.

"Six months later, Jud Sherrill called me to his office and handed me an envelope with ten thousand dollars cash in it. He said, 'Just think of it as a favor for a favor,' and winked. I realized then that was the reason he'd hired Marty as a studio gofer in the first place. To have a cop in his pocket if he should need one. I kept the money to pay Marty's way to law school.

"For twenty years now, I've thought we were home free. Then a few days ago, Sam Robbins came to see me. I don't know how he knew, or that he did for sure. But I think it's all finally over.

"So, old friend, now you know. I planned on carrying all this to the grave with me until today. Marty was here. Stephanie told him Sam had been in the house talking to me. She didn't know better—she knows nothing about what happened with Casey.

"When Marty's wife came in, I saw a bruise on her cheek. She said she fell. Like father, like son, I guess. He wouldn't listen when I told him to get help.

"Sam told me he sees you on occasion. I thought about telling him all this myself but felt I owed an explanation to you first."

Schaefer let out another long sigh. "I guess that's it." After a lengthy pause, he said, "Good-bye, old friend."

"You still there?" Jake said over the phone.

"Yeah. Have you called Bracken?"

"Not yet. I wanted you to hear it first."

After we said good-bye, I found Sam's tape recorder and listened to the tape Macie had inadvertently kept safe for me. In it Sam was talking to himself, trying to figure everything out.

"Definitely dirty," he said as the tape rolled. "Mrs. Frazier corroborated Douglas Anne's story of Casey's crush on Sherrill. Seeing her pictures reminded me how much Casey and Stephanie looked alike back then.

"What was that old guy's name? The neighbor of the Schaefers? He told me he saw Stephanie on her bike the day in question. But when he found out she was at work all day, he apologized. Said he must have gotten the days mixed up, that his memory wasn't what it used to be. What if he saw Casey instead, riding to Stephanie's house?

"Hmm. Let's say it *was* Casey. She rides by her friend's

— 182 —

house. Nobody's home—they're all at work, right? Not right. Somebody was there. Suppose Martin Jr.'s alibi was fixed. He could've gone home for lunch. The other boys could've been with him.

"Casey stops in. They're alone, but she's not afraid. She trusts them and she still has a crush on Blaine. Maybe she flirts a little. Things get out of hand, turn ugly . . . ."

Another silence stretched out on the tape. Sam didn't speak for so long I reached out, thinking that must be all of it. "Doesn't jive," he said finally. "Boys had tight alibis. No evidence that either they or Casey had been at the house. No witnesses to put them together. Also, her body showed no sign of movement after death. She was done at the scene.

"Unless . . . they drive her there. She says, 'I'm on the way to the park.' They say, 'Throw your bike in, we'll give you a ride.' There's a little cuddling in the back . . . the driver pulls over in the woods. That would fit."

Another pause stretched out on the tape. "That's a great story. Too bad you can't prove a damn bit of it," he said to himself. "It's time to let Willi in on it. Tell her everything, about me, about Casey. I'll tell her about Jake tonight, too. Between the three of us, maybe we can figure out the next step." Sam blew out another long sigh before cutting off the machine. I did the same, pressing the STOP button.

For the next two days, I stayed home. Except for letting Ralph and Lucille know I was okay, checking up on Macie, and a few phone conversations with Bracken, I talked with no one. This wasn't entirely due to my lack of motivation. Bracken had given me strict orders to keep quiet.

The newspaper ran a front-page story the morning after Macie's shooting. I doubt it was because anyone cared about a helpless old lady. More likely, it was because of the arrest of a prominent local attorney. In the story, my part in it all wasn't quite accurate. They credited me as one of Macie's "rescuers" and as "a private eye affiliated with Robbins Investigations."

On the third day, I was still pretty dazed from it all but I managed to get out in the world. After stopping by Ralph and Lucille's for lunch, I left Buddy in their backyard for the rest of the day. I wanted to spend some time at Sam's place to finish up the last bit of packing and storing.

The answering machine's red light blinked rapidly on his desk. Aside from a reporter who called twice, the remaining twelve messages were people who saw the newspaper article and wanted to hire me. I made a list of their names and numbers so I could call back and politely decline their business.

Late that afternoon, after carrying the last box of files up to the third floor of Ralph's building, I looked out the window over the old sink, ancient and naked, that Sam used for developing photos. I leaned on it, the only fixture in the room, enjoying the view of the wild signs painted on the tattoo parlor/junk store down below. Behind it, a slight breeze blew up a country song, too light to recognize, from The Club Car's open door.

At lunch, Uncle Ralph had tried to talk me into taking over Sam's business. He kept talking about what good money I could make. He even said he'd help on stakeouts. When I still didn't act like I wanted to do it, he said I could have the place rent-free for as long as I needed it.

I didn't tell him the truth—how much I loved it here. How this view from Sam's world appealed to me. Being in this part of town, in this building, gave me a sense of belonging. It was a lot like the way I felt playing with Melvin's band, like I had come back to myself after being lost.

During my years up here in the music business I hadn't felt lost. As I looked back, though, it was as if I remembered another person's life. Someone wandering around with plenty of money, plenty of friends, and absolutely no clue that her work was eating away something important inside, leaving her hollow and lonely.

Sam had changed that for me. Even with him gone, I felt more comfort here with nothing but dust and his ghost than anywhere I'd lived.

Avoiding the thought that I'd soon be leaving here forever, I sifted through a tray of pictures next to the sink. Finding one very much like the one on Macie's altar, I wiped it off and took it with me downstairs. For a long time I lay on Sam's couch, staring at the snapshot while listening to the rush-hour street noise below.

When the phone rang, I ignored it at first. The gruff voice leaving a message made me change my mind. I jumped off the couch and ran to see what news Bracken had for me.

"Just wanted to let you know the latest developments," he said. "L.A. officers have obtained the necklace. They verify on the middle bead, the word *Forever* is clearly inscribed. As soon as we received their notification, we moved on the other two suspects. Blaine Sherrill and Rick Crawford are both in custody."

"Good work, detective," I said. "Have you told Stephanie?"

"Not yet. I'm going over later with a social worker. She handled the idea of her brother's possible guilt and of finding Casey's necklace pretty well the other day. Still, I want to be sure someone is there with me who can help her if she needs it."

After we hung up, I felt restless. Deciding I needed a good walk, I grabbed my purse and stuck the keys in the front door lock. Just as I pulled the door to, the phone rang again. I stared at it through the second ring. Thinking Bracken might have forgotten something, I was about to pick up when Jill began leaving her message.

"Willi, I'm calling to inform you that, thanks to you, Jennalyn Wade has canceled us on the live shows and the cable TV special in Los Angeles. *Us*, Willi. *All* of us. That's *five thousand dollars* you've taken from me and Luanne! I *needed* that money for my kids!

"Jen said her lawyer advised her not to have any contact with you but wouldn't tell me why. All this stuff about Jud is true, isn't it? What else have you done? Why is she talking to her lawyer about you?

"Whatever it is, congratulations. You've ruined any chance that we'll ever work for either of them again. That's it, Willi. From now on, I won't be calling you for work with me and Luanne. You can find your own damn sessions."

She slammed the phone down. As the machine reset, I took one last look inside and locked the office, feeling as if the doors were closing on both my worlds.

On the way back from the drugstore, I walked in front of St. Ann's church. A children's choir sang inside. Intending only to listen near the open doors, I couldn't keep myself from getting closer and closer until I wound up going in.

Crossing the foyer, I stood at the back of the sanctuary. A lady carrying a bucket of cleaning supplies walked toward the front and out the side door, leaving me alone downstairs. I couldn't see the choir from where I stood but could hear them above me in the loft.

None of the recessed lights high in the ceiling were on over the worship area. Only in the loft were fluorescents turned on to augment the daylight slanting in the windows. The nave had a soft source of light, that of about a dozen candles underneath a statue of Mary.

The cleaning lady returned to the chapel without her supplies. After touching her finger to the holy water, she made the sign of the cross as she passed in front of the altar. Lighting a candle on the marble shelf at Mary's feet, she turned and sat down to pray.

Her lips moved as she held her rosary. Its beads fell around her hand one by one, becoming blue to my eyes as I counted fifteen years and contemplated the sorrowful mystery of Casey's death.

With Sam's musings still running through my head, I could see how Casey's necklace could have survived unbroken. It was the flirting. She had a crush on him. She and Blaine would've talked about their trip to Paris; she might show him the necklace she'd bought there. Perhaps he asked her to take it off for a closer look, then teased her, stuffed it in his jeans pocket, and forgot about it.

Jennalyn said she caught the boys as they were about to throw it away. They had to come up with a story, and told her they found it at the Ryman where they'd been working. They saw no harm in giving it to Jen, knowing she'd be leaving town soon.

Mary's candles glowed brighter as dusk settled in. It would be dark outside soon. On the way out, I noticed the statues on either side of the doors. Both of them, St. Joseph and St. Ann, had empty shelves. I lit a candle at the feet of St. Joseph, the patron of fathers and protectors. Perhaps if someone had knelt here twenty years ago to bring down help for Jud Sherrill and Martin Schaefer Sr., the fathers might have had the courage for justice.

And Sam would be alive if not for the precious sons. "The most precious thing . . . the only thing," Stephanie had said, encapsulating the dark truth of our world. The precious sons had raped, murdered, lied, and prospered. *Whose side were you on, Joe?*

St. Ann stood patiently in the dark. The sun was almost gone now with only the hope before Joseph lighting the back of the chapel. I lit a candle on St. Ann's shelf and studied the serenity and gentleness in her face. I promised myself I'd come back often, to keep her corner lit, to keep her kind, loving features visible, even when nobody looked or cared.

I could hear the choir dismissing above me. Before they came down, I stepped out into the night. As I walked, I thought about Jill's message. As much as I wanted to call to explain, I knew I couldn't. It might jeopardize the case. Even when all the facts started emerging, she wouldn't forgive me easily. And not for a long time.

The three of us had enjoyed a good run in the music business. Ninety-nine percent of those who try to get studio work can't; those who do rarely have the steady income we've had so many years. We never talked about it, but we knew female singers over forty only got road work. I didn't know of any still doing sessions in Nashville. Even without losing work because of Jud, I know it would've soon started dwindling anyway.

Nearing the cross street between the tattoo parlor and Ralph's building, I could hear The Club Car's jukebox around the corner. I almost turned left to have a beer but changed my mind because I couldn't stand the song they were playing. In country music, there's a very thin line between a good

song and a real cowpie-smellin', tobacco-drippin', stupid one.

As I stepped off the curb, I took in a deep breath of freedom. There *was* one upside to all this. Unless I felt like it, or desperately needed the money, I'd never have to sit through another bad country session again. I made up my mind to touch base with the few producers in town who did rhythm-and-blues records. Maybe even take a trip down to the Shoals to try to drum up some business. In the meantime, I would need some other source of income.

Taking the steps up to Sam's office, I wondered how long it would take to get a private investigator's license. With the list of names and phone numbers I'd taken off the answering machine that afternoon, I'd at least have somewhere to start.

Once inside, I reached into my bag of goodies from the drugstore, took out two candles, and set them on the desk. With the wicks lit and the overhead light off, I took the picture of Sam and Macie I'd found upstairs and leaned it against the tape player. Not as elaborate as Macie's altar, but it would do. As my mind cleared in the stillness, my confession rose up inside me.

*I'm Macie.* Maybe I don't wear cat-eye glasses or walk the streets talking to myself, but I'm just as wandering and lost, just as much a thief wishing for trinkets from a man I can't have.

When my eyes became so blurry I could hardly see, I reached over and pushed PLAY, just to hear his voice. Laying my head on the desk near the speaker, I pressed my cheek against the cool wood.

His words were like a soft caress, a comforting hand brushing over my hair, the candles' heat like a warm kiss on my forehead. I imagined his lips gently resting there in the darkness. With a fervent prayer of thanks, I remembered each gift, pulling them up one by one like Macie reaching in her purse and saying, *He gave me this. He gave me this.*